"I'm simply here to inform you that you will have a child in approximately six months, and to discuss options for its care." Ivy hoped she sounded calm.

She continued, "As I told you, I don't have the means to care for a child. I offered to be Connie's surrogate on the understanding that she would then take the child after he or she was born. I didn't envisage..." She stopped, a strange feeling constricting inside her, part grief and part an aching fear that she didn't quite understand. "What I mean to say is that the child isn't mine. Or at least, I don't view it as such. It's always been Connie's."

The sheikh's gaze ran over her, suddenly very intense, making her breath catch and foreboding twist hard in her gut.

"You said you didn't want a family," he said almost thoughtfully. "Why is that?"

Ivy blinked at the change of subject. "That's really none of your business."

He lifted one black brow. "Is it not? You're pregnant with my child, which makes this very much my business."

The words *pregnant with my child* made her feel warm, her cheeks heating. How ridiculous to blush about something like that, especially when it wasn't what it sounded like and they both knew it.

Jackie Ashenden writes dark, emotional stories with alpha heroes who've just gotten the world to their liking only to have it blown apart by their kick-ass heroines. She lives in Auckland, New Zealand, with her husband, the inimitable Dr. Jax, two kids and two rats. When she's not torturing alpha males and their gutsy heroines, she can be found drinking chocolate martinis, reading anything she can lay her hands on, wasting time on social media or being forced to go mountain biking with her husband. To keep up-to-date with Jackie's new releases and other news, sign up to her newsletter at jackieashenden.com.

Books by Jackie Ashenden

Harlequin Presents

Visit the Author Profile page
at Harlequin.com for more titles.

Jackie Ashenden

THE INNOCENT
CARRYING HIS LEGACY

HARLEQUIN
PRESENTS

Recycling programs
for this product may
not exist in your area.

ISBN-13: 978-1-335-56779-6

The Innocent Carrying His Legacy

Copyright © 2021 by Jackie Ashenden

All rights reserved. No part of this book may be used or reproduced in
any manner whatsoever without written permission except in the case of
brief quotations embodied in critical articles and reviews.

This is a work of fiction. Names, characters, places and incidents
are either the product of the author's imagination or are used fictitiously.
Any resemblance to actual persons, living or dead, businesses,
companies, events or locales is entirely coincidental.

This edition published by arrangement with Harlequin Books S.A.

For questions and comments about the quality of this book,
please contact us at CustomerService@Harlequin.com.

Harlequin Enterprises ULC
22 Adelaide St. West, 40th Floor
Toronto, Ontario M5H 4E3, Canada
www.Harlequin.com

Printed in U.S.A.

THE INNOCENT
CARRYING HIS LEGACY

This one's for Lily.

CHAPTER ONE

'SHE'S STILL THERE, SIR.'

Sheikh Nazir Al Rasul, owner of one of the most powerful and most discreet private armies in the world, and a warrior to his bones, gave his guard a hard stare. The guard was young, a boy still, but he wore his black and gold uniform with pride and his shoulders were squared with determination.

Admirable. But Nazir had left strict instructions that he wasn't to be disturbed. He'd just returned to Inaris after a particularly delicate operation involving putting down a coup in one of the Baltic states and, after two days of no sleep, he was in no mood to have his orders disobeyed by wet-behind-the-ears guards.

Nazir lifted his chin slightly—always a warning sign to his officers. 'Did I say I was to be disturbed?' He didn't raise his voice. He didn't need to.

The young soldier blanched. 'No, sir.'

'Then explain your presence. Immediately.'

The boy shifted on his feet.

Nazir stared.

With an effort the boy stilled. 'You said to let you know if anything changed.'

Nazir was tired and so it took a moment for the statement to penetrate. And then it did.

The guard was talking about the uninvited guest who'd turned up outside the gates of Nazir's fortress. That wasn't unusual—many people made the trek to his fortress in the middle of the desert. They braved the terrible rumours he'd put about on purpose to discourage visitors, wanting either to join his army or seek his assistance, or request his tutelage. He was a master in the art of war, especially physical combat, and his expertise was well known and sought after.

He refused everyone who turned up at his gates, which, alas, didn't stop people from turning up.

However, they were usually male. This time it was a woman.

She'd appeared several hours ago along with a local guide, who should have known better.

Nazir didn't let anyone into his fortress and he didn't want to start now, and so he'd given his guards strict instructions to ignore the woman. Usually people went away after the first couple of hours. Waiting outside the gates in the brutal desert sun was a more effective deterrent than any number of dogs or weapons.

Irritation settled in Nazir's gut, but he ignored it. A good commander never let either his emotions or physical discomfort affect him, and Nazir was a good commander. No, he was an excellent commander.

'What's changed?' he demanded without any discernible change of tone.

The guard hesitated a second. 'Well…ah…it appears that she's pregnant, sir.'

Nazir stared, this time not taking it in at all. 'Pregnant? What do you mean she's pregnant?'

The guard opened his mouth. Shut it. Lifted a shoulder. Then seemed to collect himself and stood straighter. 'She asked for water and a…sun umbrella. Because she was pregnant, she said.'

Nazir didn't blink, not even at the mention of a sun umbrella. 'She's lying,' he said flatly. 'Do nothing.'

'Sir. She had…uh…' The guard made a curving gesture in the region of his stomach. 'We could see it on the camera.'

Nazir had had two nights without sleep. He'd just overseen an operation that had required some delicacy, and he already had requests for his services from the governments of two nations, in addition to a number of private enquiries, and what he desperately needed right now was sleep. Not to deal with yet another idiot turning up at his gates wanting God only knew what. Especially a pregnant idiot.

'Do nothing,' he repeated. 'Letting her in will only encourage more of these fools. And as to her being pregnant, that's easy enough to fake.'

'Sir, she's asking for you by name.'

Nazir was not moved. 'Yes, they all do.' Though admittedly, that did not include pregnant women. The likelihood of him siring a child was, after all, close to zero since he was always careful when it came to sex and even then he didn't indulge himself often. Giving in to those baser, more physical instincts made a man soft.

Voices drifted down the echoing stone hallway and then came the sound of running feet. Another young guard appeared, looking excited. He came to a stop outside Nazir's bedroom door, clicked his heels together smartly and stood at attention. 'Sir,' he said breathlessly. 'The woman has fainted.'

Of course she had. It was clearly too much to ask that he had an uninterrupted couple of hours' sleep. Clearly it was also too much to ask that his men ignore her. They didn't get much in the way of female company, it was true, but if all it took was one woman turning up at the gates to generate this much excitement, then it was apparent that either his men needed more and harder drills, or some leave was in order.

It was also apparent that he was not going to get any sleep until the issue with the woman had been dealt with.

'Bring her to the guardhouse,' Nazir ordered tersely, letting no hint of his temper show. 'I'll deal with her there.'

Both guards saluted and disappeared off up the corridor.

Nazir muttered a curse under his breath then grabbed the black robe he'd hung over the back of a chair, belting it loosely around his waist before striding out.

This was the very last thing he needed right now.

There were always people coming to his gates, but

he never let them in and he didn't particularly want to start now. Especially not with a woman who'd demanded first a sun umbrella then fainted. She was probably some idiot tourist who'd heard the rumours he'd carefully cultivated to deter most of the people who turned up at his door—rumours about the brutal warlord and his army of murdering thugs that he'd collected from prisons around the world, who led a nomadic lifestyle in the desert to escape detection and woe betide any who came across them because they did not understand the concept of mercy.

It was the best kind of rumour, one that held grains of truth. He *was* a brutal warlord and it wasn't that he didn't understand mercy, he just saw no point to it. The murdering thugs and the nomadic lifestyle were smokescreens, naturally, but it succeeded in deterring most idle fools.

This woman was clearly a fool who had not been deterred.

One thing he was sure of though: she definitely wasn't pregnant. And if she was then she was more of a fool than he'd initially thought. What woman would head out into the middle of the desert in search of him, despite the terrible rumours, then spend a couple of hours standing outside his gates in the sun, and all while she was pregnant?

Nazir strode out of the big stone fortress he called home and across the dusty courtyard in front of it, heading towards the small guardhouse by the massive reinforced steel gates.

It was a sturdy building made of stone, equipped

with the same high-tech surveillance equipment that was in use in the rest of the compound. It was also air-conditioned—unlike the fortress, which didn't need it due to its medieval construction of thick stone walls that protected from the worst of the heat—since the heat was brutal and Nazir preferred his men un-cooked, especially when on guard duty.

The two guards outside saluted at his approach and Nazir ran a reflexive, critical eye over them. Guards on duty in the hottest part of the day were relieved on the hour every hour, and, judging by the colour of these two, they were due to be relieved any min-ute. They were also new recruits, young men want-ing to prove themselves to him, which often led to unwanted complications.

'Make sure you get some water when you go off-duty,' he said shortly. 'Soldiers who can't look after themselves are of no use to me.'

'Yes, sir,' the two guards said as one.

Nazir pulled open the heavy iron door into the guardhouse and stepped inside.

Another guard stood near the door while a sec-ond sat at the station in front of the bank of screens and computers that constantly monitored all areas of the fortress.

The downside of being Commander of one of the world's most sought-after and feared private armies was that he'd made many, many enemies. And there were a great many people who wanted him and his army gone. Preferably for ever.

His fortress was marked on no maps, nor was it

detectable via any other high-tech search, and all its communications were encrypted. To the rest of the world it simply didn't exist. Yet there were always people trying to find it and trying to find him.

They always failed.

The beauty of the desert was that it mostly did his work for him when it came to winnowing out his enemies.

Of course, there were always a few determined souls who didn't let sand and savage heat stop them.

Souls such as the woman who lay in a bundle of dirty white robes on a makeshift camp stretcher set up on the guardhouse floor.

The two guards came to attention the instant Nazir stepped inside.

He ignored them, moving over to the camp stretcher where the woman lay.

She was small, her figure and hair obscured by the robes she wore, which had obviously been bought from the tourist bazaar in Mahassa since the cotton was thin and cheap and would offer exactly zero protection from the sun. Her hair was covered by another length of cotton, but her face was unveiled. She had a pointed chin, a small nose, and straight dark brows. There was an almost feline cast to her features, not pretty in the least, but her mouth was fairly arresting. It was full and pouty and sensual, though her lips were cracked.

Her lashes were thick and silky-looking, lying still on sunburned cheeks…

Actually no, they weren't still. They were quivering slightly and Nazir could detect a faint, pale gleam from underneath them.

An odd, delicious thrill went through him, though what it was and what it meant, he couldn't have said. What he did know was that the woman was definitely not unconscious.

And she was watching him.

Ivy Dean had been on the point of pretending to wake up when the door to the small guardhouse she'd been taken to had opened and the tallest, broadest man she'd ever seen had walked in.

Her breath had caught and the fear she hadn't felt once during the long and sometimes frustrating journey from England's cool, misty rain to the brutal heat of Inaris had suddenly come rushing over her.

Because it wasn't just his height—which had to be well over six three—or the fact that he was built like a rugby prop forward, or maybe more accurately an ancient Roman gladiator. No, it was the aura he projected, which she felt like a change in air pressure as soon as he entered the guardhouse.

Danger. Sheer, heart-pumping, terrifying danger.

He radiated a kind of leashed, savage violence, like a dragon guarding his hoard.

And she was the rabbit served up to him for his lunch.

She stayed very still on the camp bed they'd laid her on, holding her breath and silently regretting her decision to fake a faint as he loomed over her, because no doubt he'd pick up on her play-acting easily enough. He was just the kind of man who saw everything, including pretence.

Through the veil of her lashes, she caught a glimpse of a face that looked as if it had been carved from solid granite. His nose was crooked, his cheekbones carved, his jaw square and sharp. His chiselled mouth was as hard as the rest of his features and what could have been sensual had firmed into a grim line.

It was a harsh face, intensely masculine and not pretty in the slightest.

His eyes were what truly terrified her, though. Because they were the most astonishing colour, a bright clear turquoise framed by thick black lashes. She'd seen eyes that colour in the tourist bazaar of Mahassa, in the faces of people descended from the ancient nomadic desert tribes, and they were unusual and beautiful.

But in the face of this man, the colour had frozen and turned as icy as the tundra in the north. There was no mercy in those eyes. No kindness. No warmth.

There was death in those eyes.

This was the warlord, wasn't it? The one she'd followed all those rumours about. The terrifying, cruel Sheikh who lived in the desert with an army of murderers who either stole people away to sell in some black-market trafficking ring, or killed them where they stood.

'Stay away from the desert, miss,' the staff at the tourism information centre had told her. 'No one goes into the desert.'

They didn't understand though. She *had* to go into

the desert. Because it was the warlord she had to find. Even though she hadn't wanted to. Even though it went against every self-protective urge she had.

She had to at least try, for Connie's sake.

The warlord stared at her, the expression on his harsh face utterly unforgiving, and Ivy's mouth went bone dry. Unable to stop herself, she slid a protective hand over the slight roundness of her stomach.

His predator's gaze flickered as he spotted the movement and abruptly he straightened to his full height, looking down at her.

'You can stop pretending now,' he said in perfect, accentless English. 'I know you're awake.'

His voice was as deep and as harsh as his features, like an earthquake rumbling under the ground, and he issued it not so much as an observation but as a command.

He was a man used to giving orders, which made sense. Authority radiated from him, the kind of authority that came without arrogance, the kind that was innate. The kind of authority that some people were simply born with.

Ivy found herself stirring and opening her eyes before she'd even registered that she was doing so.

The warlord said nothing, his frozen gaze taking in every inch of her as she sat up, making it obvious that the onus was on her to explain herself.

Fear gathered like a kernel of ice in her stomach and she kept her hand where it was, as if she could protect the small life inside her not only from the man standing in front of her, but from her fear as well.

But giving in to such emotions was never helpful and despite the urging of her primitive lizard brain to make a dash for the door, throw it open, and run for her life, she remained where she was. Being practical was key; she wouldn't get far even if she did run, not in a fortress full of soldiers. And besides, where would she run to? There was nothing but desert outside, her guide having abandoned her as soon as he realised that she had no intention of merely viewing the fortress from a safe distance, that she actually wanted to go inside and speak to the warlord himself.

Anyway, show no fear. That was what you had to do when faced with a predator. Running would only get you eaten.

Ivy ignored the ice inside her, just as she ignored that, even from a few feet away, the man still managed to loom over her, making the guardhouse feel ten times smaller than it actually was.

'I should thank you,' Ivy began coolly. 'For your—'

'Your name and purpose,' the man cut across her in that rough, rumbling voice, his tone making it clear that this was not a request in any way.

Okay, so if he was indeed Sheikh Nazir Al Rasul, the infamous warlord—and she had a sneaking suspicion he might be—then she would have to tread delicately here.

But she also wouldn't allow herself to be intimidated. Back in England, she managed an entire children's home full of foster kids, some of them with quite severe behavioural and mental-health issues, and she had no difficulty keeping them in order.

One man, no matter how tall and terrifying, was not going to get the better of her.

'Very well,' she said. 'My name is Ivy Dean. I've registered my whereabouts with the British Consulate in Mahassa and they know exactly where I am.' She forced herself to meet the man's terrifyingly cold eyes. 'And if I don't return within a few days, they'll also know exactly why.'

He said nothing, continuing to pin her where she sat on the edge of the camp bed with that icy stare, his face betraying no expression whatsoever.

Fine.

'I'm here because I need to speak with Sheikh Nazir Al Rasul,' she continued, determinedly holding his gaze. 'It concerns a private matter.'

The man stood so still he might have been carved from desert rock. 'What private matter?'

'That's between me and Mr Al Rasul.'

'Tell me.' There was no discernible change in tone from anything else he'd said, but if his other statements had been orders, this was a command. One that he clearly expected her to obey without question.

She should have been cowed. Any other woman in her right mind would be, especially after standing for hours in the hot sun outside the gates of a desert fortress, waiting to speak with one of the most terrifying men she'd ever heard about.

But Ivy hadn't spent more than two weeks in Mahassa trying to find a guide who would take her into the desert in search of the mysterious warlord for nothing. She'd spent all her meagre savings trying to find this man and she wasn't going to give up now, especially when she was so close to her goal.

In fact, if her suspicions were correct, then her goal was standing right in front of her.

Except, she needed to know he was indeed the man she'd been searching for. Because if he wasn't, this could end up going very badly, not only for her but also for the baby she was currently carrying.

Ivy folded her hands calmly in her lap, pulling on the same practical, steely mask that she used with the most recalcitrant boys in the home. 'I'll speak with Mr Al Rasul,' she said firmly. 'As I said, it's a private matter.'

Again, there was no discernible change of expression in his icy gaze and he didn't move. Yet it felt as if the atmosphere in the guardhouse abruptly chilled. The two guards standing at attention became very still, their agitation apparent.

Apparently it was not done to disobey this man.

A tremor of fear moved through Ivy at the same time as she felt something else, something unfamiliar, flicker in her bloodstream. A small thrill. Which didn't make any sense. She was a woman alone in a fortress full of men who could kill her easily. And no matter how confidently she'd talked about the British Consulate, they couldn't exactly help her right now if things went south.

Which they might, if the rumours about the man in front of her were true.

So there was no reason at all for her to feel the smallest twinge of excitement, of...anticipation? The thrill of matching wits with someone as strong-willed and determined as she. Maybe even stronger.

Perhaps it was the pregnancy doing strange things to her. Why, she'd just been talking to Connie the other day about—

Connie.

An echo of grief pulsed through her, but she forced it away. No, now was not the time. Connie's last wish had been to find Mr Al Rasul, and so that was what she was going to do. Then she could grieve her friend properly, once this was all over.

'Perhaps you did not understand,' the man said with icy precision. 'You'll tell me. Now.'

Ivy refused to be cowed. 'This is for Mr Al Rasul's ears alone.'

Something dangerous glinted in his eyes. 'I am Mr Al Rasul.'

Of course he was. Somehow she'd known that the second he'd spotted her faking a faint.

Still, one couldn't be sure. And she had to be very, *very* certain about this.

'Prove it,' Ivy said.

The atmosphere, already chilly, plunged a few thousand degrees and the two guards' stares abruptly became very fixed. They were statue still, like rabbits being eyed by a hawk.

The icy kernel in Ivy's gut got larger, sending out cold tendrils of fear to weave through her veins.

Why are you challenging him like this? Are you insane?

That could very well be. Perhaps she had sunstroke or was on the verge of extreme dehydration. Perhaps the last few days in Mahassa, spent following up leads only to end up in frustrating dead ends and brick walls, had got to her. Perhaps she was now hallucinating.

Still, she couldn't back down. Not when the child inside her depended on her. And if she could stare down a bunch of sullen teenage boys who'd been caught shoplifting, then she could certainly hold out against one infamous desert warlord.

Sullen teenage boys aren't likely to kill you.

That was very true. Though it was too late now.

The man's cold, flat stare didn't shift from her, not once. And he didn't blink. She couldn't read him at all.

Then he inclined his head minutely and the guard on his left abruptly rattled off in heavily accented English. 'You are speaking with the Commander, Sheikh Nazir Al Rasul.'

'That's your proof?' Ivy couldn't help saying. 'One of your guards who is clearly terrified of you?'

'That is all the proof you will be getting,' Al Rasul said. 'I am not accustomed to repeating myself, but in this case you're obviously having difficulty understanding me.' His gaze became sharper, more intensely focused, and Ivy's breath froze as the expressionless mask dropped and she caught a glimpse of what it had been hiding.

Death. Chaos. Violence. Danger.

This man was a killer.

'You will tell me your purpose here,' he went on expressionlessly. 'Or I'll have you thrown out before the gates and you can find your own way back to the city.'

It was a death sentence and they both knew it.

This time it was harder to force down her fear and when she reflexively smoothed her robe over her stomach, her hands shook. 'Very well,' she said with as much calm as she could muster. 'But as I said, it's a private matter.'

'You need not concern yourself with my guards.'

Good. She needed to get this over with and the sooner the better.

Ivy took a breath, steeled herself, then met his ferocious gaze. 'I'm pregnant. And I'm here to inform you that the child is yours.'

CHAPTER TWO

AN ICY BOLT of shock flickered through Nazir. Then his logic took over.

She was lying, for what reason he couldn't possibly imagine, but she was. When he indulged himself with a woman, he was always scrupulous with protection. Children would never be in his future. He didn't want them. He'd been brought up to be a soldier and that was his life, and the domesticity of a wife and children had no place in that life.

Apart from anything else, he remembered every woman he slept with and he definitely had *not* slept with the one sitting on the camp bed in front of him, with her hands in her lap and absolutely no fear at all in her clear, copper-coloured eyes.

He would have laughed if he remembered how.

'Leave us,' he ordered calmly to the two guards, virtually quivering in their eagerness to be out of the guardhouse. There was no need for them to waste precious time listening to this woman's nonsense.

They exited the building like racehorses leaping out of the starting gate.

The woman—Ivy Dean—didn't move a muscle and she didn't look away.

No, she wasn't someone he'd ever take to bed. She was small, with a delicacy to her that would make the rough sex he particularly enjoyed unworkable. He preferred warrior women. Women he didn't have to worry about accidentally hurting, who could hold their own in bed and out of it.

Yet, he couldn't deny that there had been something almost…intriguing about her refusal to obey him. Or the way that little pointed chin of hers had lifted in stubborn protest at his orders.

Sadly, though, no matter how stubborn she was, he was in command here and even though she wasn't a physical threat to him, she might be a threat in other ways. He had many enemies—including whole countries—and someone might be using her to get to him. It was a novel approach, but nothing could be dismissed and this—she—was deeply suspicious.

Which meant he had to find out the real reason she was here come hell or high water.

'You're lying,' he said expressionlessly.

'I'm not,' she shot back.

'Prove it.' He didn't consciously imitate her; he didn't need to.

Her pretty mouth pursed in displeasure at having that thrown back at her. Then she sniffed. 'Very well.'

She slipped off the camp bed and stood up, only to sway a little, suddenly unsteady on her feet. It seemed that regardless of whether she'd been faking that faint or not, the wait outside in the hot sun hadn't been kind to her.

The boy he'd once been would have been concerned about that, but the man had no room in his heart for concern. So it came as somewhat of a surprise to him that he found himself reaching forward to take her elbow to steady her.

She gave a soft little intake of breath and froze like a gazelle under the paw of a lion. The sound of her gasp echoed in the small room and he felt it echo inside him, too. She felt very warm and, despite the sharp angles of her face, very soft.

It's been years since you've had soft... A lifetime...

Disturbed by his reaction, Nazir let her go. Strange to find himself...affected in such a way. He had perfect control over himself and his impulses and he wasn't accustomed to having a physical reaction he wasn't in complete command over.

Perhaps it was simply weariness. He really did need some sleep.

Ivy moved away from him very quickly, as if she couldn't wait to put some distance between them, heading for the battered leather bag that sat against the desk in the corner. She must have been carrying it with her when they'd brought her in.

She moved over to it, the dirty white robe pooling around her as she bent to pick it up, rummaging around for something inside it. A moment later, she pulled out a sheaf of papers that she turned and brandished at him.

'Here,' she said, her voice light and sweet with a distinct undercurrent of iron. 'Your proof.'

Nazir took the papers and glanced down at them.

On the top was a printout from a fertility clinic in England and on it, in very clear black and white, were his physical and personal details, including his name. There was also a set of paternity test results, and what looked to be a personal note in shaky handwriting.

Ice gripped him.

It had been a long time ago, when he'd had those three years at Cambridge University. Away from his father's iron grip, away from the palace and its rules and strictures. He hadn't wanted to go initially, because he'd known he was being given a punishment, not freedom, yet his father had been insistent. He'd had no choice but to go. So he had, deciding that if it was a punishment, then it was a punishment he'd enjoy the hell out of. He'd been eighteen and full of passion, determined to take life by the throat and experience everything he could, and that was exactly what he'd done.

He'd always known he'd never be a father, that a family life wasn't possible for him. As the bastard son of the Sultana—the secret bastard son— he couldn't be allowed to further taint the royal line with offspring.

That had burned, even back then, even when he'd been too young for a family. So one night, drunk with some of his friends and making stupid bets over poker, he'd lost a bet that had involved sperm donation. They'd only been boys, unthinking and stupid, but even then a part of him had felt a certain savage pleasure. That somewhere there'd be a child of his despite all the rules his father had set.

Then he'd returned to Inaris and, in the aftermath of everything that had happened, he'd forgotten about it.

Until now.

There was no disputing the facts. The evidence was clear in the papers he held, and even if there had been a chance that they'd been forged, he knew they hadn't been.

He knew the truth.

Carefully, Nazir folded up the papers and put them into the pocket of his combat trousers. The woman opened her mouth to protest, but then took one look at his face and shut it again.

A wise decision.

'Sit,' he ordered tersely.

She didn't protest that either, moving to the chair at the watch station and sitting down.

'Explain,' Nazir commanded. 'Leave out nothing.'

She took a breath, her small pink tongue coming out and touching her lower lip briefly. He found himself watching it for no good reason.

'I need some water first,' she said, apparently not understanding that his tone meant he was to be obeyed and immediately.

'No,' he said.

One straight brow arched. 'Excuse me? I was forced to stand outside your gates in the desert heat, with no shade or water—'

'I don't care.'

'And I'm pregnant.' She ignored the interruption. 'With your child.'

Nazir stared at her. She was challenging him, no doubt about it, matching his will with hers—or at least, attempting to. And part of him had to admit to a certain reluctant admiration at the sheer gall of her. No one challenged him, except for his enemies and those with a death wish. Which was she?

She's right, though. She is carrying your child.

He glanced down at her stomach before he could stop himself, the slight curve veiled by the dusty white robes she wore. Something raw and hot and primitive stirred inside him in response.

He ignored it.

'Water,' he said.

'Yes, please.' She clasped long, delicate fingers together in her lap. 'A small glass would do.'

Well, if it was water she wanted, then water she would receive.

Nazir strode over to the door, pulled it open, and spoke briefly to the guards outside, then shut it again and turned back to where she sat, small and precise and utterly self-contained.

She met his gaze squarely, though he thought he detected a slight hint of wariness. Which was good and proved she had some intelligence after all. Because she should be wary. It was clear she was used to having her own way, but she would not get it here.

This was his fortress and he ruled it with an iron fist.

He folded his arms and stood in front of her, holding her coppery gaze with his own.

And waited.

'I'll need water first before any explanations,' she said.

'Indeed.'

Another moment or two passed.

She shifted restively but didn't look away. 'If you're trying to intimidate me, Mr Al Rasul, it won't work.'

'I'm not trying to intimidate you,' he said. 'I'm merely looking at you. You'll know if I start trying to intimidate you.'

'Is that a threat?'

'Not at all. Did you take it as one?'

'It was hardly meant as anything else.'

'Good.'

She opened her mouth and closed it again.

He kept staring.

She had the most beautiful skin, very fine-grained and soft-looking, though she'd definitely caught far too much sun. Her cheeks were quite rosy, as were her forehead and chin.

You should have given her the umbrella. Especially considering she's pregnant.

The hot, primitive feeling inside him shifted again. Again, he ignored it.

No, he'd been right not to acquiesce to her demands. He had to protect this fortress and his men, which meant he couldn't afford to acknowledge random passers-by who sat outside his gates demanding water and sun umbrellas. His fortress wasn't a tourist stop.

Besides, it had been her choice to come out into the desert to find him. Clearly this was due to the pregnancy and the fact that he was the father, but there also had to be some explanation for why she'd felt the need to track him down. Whatever it was, again, that had been her decision and it had nothing to do with him.

Her eyes were pretty. In this light, the light brown coppery colour had gone almost gold, and her dark lashes looked as if they'd been brushed with the same gold. Was her hair that colour too? Was it dark? Did it have those same streaks of gold? Or was it lighter? Amber, maybe, or deep honey...

Why are you thinking about her hair?

A strange jolt went through him as he realised what he was doing. Tired, that was what he was. Too tired. There was no other reason for him to be standing there contemplating the colour of a woman's hair, especially a delicate little English rose such as this one.

A knock came on the door.

'Enter,' Nazir growled.

It opened and one of his kitchen staff came in carrying a tray. He went over to the watch station, deposited the tray on the desk, turned and then went out again.

On the tray was a very tall, elegant crystal tumbler and an elegant matching pitcher. The glass was full of ice and a clear fizzing liquid with a delicate sprig of mint as a garnish. The pitcher was full of the same liquid and ice, condensation beading the sides.

Nazir watched with interest as Ivy's pretty eyes widened, taking in the pitcher and the glass with obvious surprise.

Satisfaction flickered through him, though he ignored that too.

'That's not water,' she said, not taking her eyes off the glass.

'No, it's not,' he agreed. 'It's lemonade. It should be slightly flat since you're likely dehydrated and need some electrolytes, but choices are limited out here in the desert.'

It was obvious she didn't want to drink it; he could see it in the stubborn firming of her chin. But her lips were cracked and she was sunburned, and she had a baby to think about. And clearly her thirst was greater than her need to best him, because, after a moment, she reached for the glass and took a sip.

Her whole body shuddered and a small, helpless moan escaped her.

And just as her soft gasp had echoed through him when he'd taken her elbow before, her moan sent another echo bouncing off the walls of the emptiness inside him, the emptiness that had been there ever since he'd returned from England all those years ago, so full of righteousness and passion. So sure of himself and his position. Thinking that he was an adult now and could make his own decisions, that he wouldn't be bound by the rules of the country of his birth, and that he wanted everything that had been denied him.

And how that had led to the disappearance of his mother, the banishment of his father, and his almost execution.

No. There was a reason he was empty inside and it had to stay that way. Nothing could be permitted to fill that void except purpose and that purpose had nothing to do with a small Englishwoman and the child she carried.

Even if that child was his.

Ivy forgot about the Sheikh standing in front of her. She forgot about her fear. She forgot that she was in a desert fortress and that her elbow still felt scalded from where he'd touched it. She forgot that she was supposed to be challenging that titanic will of his, otherwise she'd certainly be crushed beneath it, and the baby along with her.

She even forgot that she'd wanted water and that that wasn't what was in the glass.

The liquid was cold and sweet, with a faintly tart edge, and it was the most delicious thing she'd ever tasted in her entire life. She took another swallow and then another, the lemonade cooling her parched throat and satisfying her thirst, yet at the same time making her realise how much thirstier she really was.

One glass wasn't going to be enough. She needed the whole pitcher.

Then powerful fingers gently but firmly disentangled hers from the glass and he took it away from her.

'No,' she protested, trying to hold onto the glass. 'I need more.'

But his strength was irresistible and she lost her hold on it, appalled to find that there were tears in her eyes as he put the glass back down on the tray next to the pitcher.

She blinked furiously, the urge to weep rushing through her like a wave. Her emotions had been all over the place with this pregnancy. She didn't normally let them run riot like this and to lose control of them in front of him, this…giant predator, Lord, how she hated it.

If he'd noticed the lapse in her control, he gave no sign.

'When you're dehydrated it's best to take small sips and often,' he said in his deep, harsh voice. 'Drinking too much and too fast will overload your kidneys.'

Ivy looked down at her hands. The flat, uninflected way he said the words was strangely calming, making the intense rush of emotion recede.

Well, it would be stupid to argue with him about the lemonade. He probably did know more about dehydration than her.

'I'm waiting,' he said.

Once more in possession of herself, Ivy glanced back up at him.

He stood in front of her, muscled arms folded across his wide chest. The black robe he wore belted around his waist had loosened, revealing the bronze skin of his throat and upper chest, and she found herself staring at it for some inexplicable reason.

It looked smooth, velvety almost, with a scattering

of crisp black hair, and she found herself wondering what it would feel like to touch it.

Why are you thinking about touching his skin?

She had no idea. It wasn't something she'd ever thought about a man before and it disturbed her.

Forcing her gaze from his chest, she glanced up at his face, ignoring the little thrill of heat that darted through her.

Not that staring at his face was any better, not with those icy eyes staring back at her, so sharp and cutting she could almost feel the edges of them scoring her.

Her mouth felt dry, more arid than the desert outside the walls of the tiny guardhouse, but she resisted the urge to grab back the glass. She'd give him the explanation he wanted, determine what he wanted re the baby, then she'd go from there.

'Okay,' she said calmly. 'So, I have…had a very dear friend of mine who desperately wanted children. She didn't have a husband or partner and so was planning to conceive via a donor. However, she was also in the middle of treatment for cancer and was unable to carry a child herself. I didn't want her to stop her treatment—she had an excellent prognosis initially—so I offered to be her surrogate. I'm not planning on having children myself and it seemed the least I could do for her.'

The warlord said nothing, no expression at all on his face.

'She agreed,' Ivy went on. 'So she picked out a donor and though she had some eggs frozen, they ended up not being viable, so we decided that she would use some of mine. It all went very well and then…' Grief caught at her throat and she had to take a second before continuing. 'The cancer became aggressive. Her treatments failed. I found out I was pregnant while she was losing her battle. I hadn't planned on having children—I have a job that makes it impossible and I don't have enough support financially—and Connie knew it. Before her death, we discussed what options there were, but we both agreed that continuing the pregnancy was important. She told me to contact the donor, to at least let him know he was a father, in case he wanted to be in the child's life. Neither of us wanted the child to have to go into foster care, but…' She stopped again, the worry and grief catching her once more despite all her efforts to contain it.

Poor Connie. She'd so desperately wanted a child and Ivy had been desperate to help her. It had been risky given Connie's illness, but both of them had tried to be optimistic. It wasn't to be, however.

Now Ivy was pregnant with a child she'd never intended to bring up herself, a child that she'd very consciously refused to think of as hers, because it wasn't. The child was Connie's, even though the genetics would prove otherwise.

Fulfilling Connie's dying wish to find the child's father had consumed her, because foster care… Well, it was an option, but not one Ivy wanted to contemplate. Not for Connie's child. She knew the effects the foster system had on kids, and though she tried to mitigate it as much as possible at the home she managed, sometimes there was no fighting a rigid system.

The man standing in front of her didn't move and there was no break at all in his expression, no lessening in the absolute focus of his gaze.

She felt like a mouse under the sharp eye of a hawk.

The urge to keep going, to keep talking to fill up the terrible silence, gripped her, but she ignored it. Instead she reached for the glass again and he made no move to stop her this time. She took a delicate sip, letting the cool liquid sit on her tongue, fighting the urge to swallow the whole lot again.

'So you came to Inaris, all the way from England. Somehow tracking down a guide who knew how to find me and then paying him no doubt an exorbitant amount of money to bring you here. Then you stand out in the hot sun for hours, enduring dehydration and putting yourself and your baby at risk so you can tell me that I have a child.' His voice was cold. 'And all for some promise to a friend?'

Ivy lifted her chin. 'She was a very close friend. And I keep my promises.'

'I am a notorious warlord, both violent and vicious. That didn't put you off? Didn't make you reflect on whether in fact I'd be someone who'd you'd want to chase up for paternal rights?' He said the words flatly, as if he had no thoughts or feelings or anything else about the fact that he was going to be a father.

Ivy took another delicate sip of lemonade then made herself put it down. True, tracking this man down hadn't been easy, but it hadn't been until she'd arrived in Inaris that she'd realised the full extent of the trouble she'd be getting herself into with him.

The rumours about him had, indeed, been terrible. And she might have given up and turned back for England then and there, because even the promise she'd made to Connie wasn't enough if the child's father was nothing but the murderer he was reputed to be.

But Connie had already pieced together some information on him when she'd found out she was terminal and had given Ivy a contact in Mahassa, the capital of Inaris. According to the contact, the rumours about the Sheikh were largely exaggerated and, though he was ruthless, he'd also been known to sometimes help those who came to him.

It wasn't much, but it was enough for Ivy to make it worth the risk. Because she wasn't only doing this for Connie, though that was a decent part of it. She was also doing it for the child. She'd grown up without a parent or a family, and it was a terrible thing; she'd seen the effects first hand in the faces of the children in the care home she managed.

'My friend had a contact who knew your approximate location and that you weren't quite as bad as the rumours would indicate.' She narrowed her gaze at him. 'Are you?'

He ignored that. 'A phone call would have been easier.'

'Yes, it would,' she said tartly, 'but when I looked

up "vicious warlord" on the Internet, there was sadly no contact information.'

He didn't smile. He didn't even blink, merely continued to stare at her in that direct way, the power of his gaze almost a physical force pushing at her.

Her jaw clenched tight. 'Mr Al Rasul—'

'You may call me "sir".'

A streak of annoyance rippled through her. 'I will do no such thing.'

'You will. I am the Commander of this fortress and my word here is law.'

'But I'm not—'

'Tell me, Miss Dean, what exactly did you expect by coming here?'

Ivy bit down on her irritation. It probably wasn't wise to challenge him, no matter how much she wanted to.

'I'm simply here to inform you that you will have a child in approximately six months, and to discuss options for its care.' She hoped she sounded calm. 'As I told you, I don't have the means to care for a child, not financially. I offered to be Connie's surrogate on the understanding that she would then take the child after he or she was born. I didn't envisage…' She stopped, a strange feeling constricting inside her, part grief and part an aching fear that she didn't quite understand. 'What I mean to say is that the child isn't mine. Or at least, I don't view it as such. It's always been Connie's.'

'Not genetically,' he pointed out.

'No, I know that. But still.' She swallowed and met his gaze squarely. 'A child should always be wanted.'

'And you do not want the child?' The question was utterly neutral.

The strange feeling inside her clutched harder. She ignored it. 'As I said, this child isn't mine. He's Connie's.'

The Sheikh's knife-bright gaze intensified all of a sudden. 'He?'

A little pulse of shock went through Ivy. That had been a slip. She'd deliberately *not* thought about the child she was carrying other than in the most basic way. She hadn't thought of names or what they would look like, or whether they'd be a boy or a girl.

It was Connie's place to do that, not hers.

But Connie is gone. And the child has no one else.

Ivy realised her hand had crept to her stomach again, resting there as if protecting the child from her own thoughts.

'He, she, I'm not sure which yet,' she said, trying to cover her lapse.

But the Sheikh didn't let her escape that easily. 'You think it's a boy, though.'

'It doesn't matter what I think.' Ivy tried to sound dismissive. 'What matters is what you would like to do as the child's father.'

The Sheikh's gaze ran over her, suddenly very intense, making her breath catch and foreboding twist hard in her gut.

'You said you didn't want a family,' he said almost thoughtfully. 'Why is that?'

Ivy blinked at the change of subject. 'That's really none of your business.'

He lifted one black brow. 'Is it not? You're pregnant with my child, which makes this very much my business.'

The words 'pregnant with my child' made her feel warm, her cheeks heating. How ridiculous to blush about something like that, especially when it wasn't what it sounded like and they both knew it.

Anyway, it seemed clear that this man probably wasn't going to be interested in caring for the child. Her quest had been a futile one.

What did you expect? That he'd offer to bring up the child? So you could offload the baby like an unwanted parcel?

The strange feeling intensified inside her, becoming an ache.

She hadn't thought about what would happen after the birth. Deliberately not thought about it, because the reality of bringing up a child she'd never expected to have was too frightening. Too confronting. She had no financial means. No family support. Yes, she managed the kids at the home, but she viewed herself as their teacher and carer, not their mother. She didn't know how to be a mother, not when she'd never had one of her own.

No, she would be totally alone.

Besides, how could she when managing the home took up so much of her time? How could she give a child the attention it needed and deserved when she had so many other deserving children to watch over?

Don't think about it. One step at a time.

Ivy forced away the steadily rising panic, slipping off the camp bed and getting to her feet. 'It's clearly not business you're interested in, however,' she said with icy calm. 'A fortress full of men commanded by a warlord is hardly the place for a child anyway. Thank you for taking the time to see me. If you could spare me someone to take me back to Mahassa that would be appreciated.'

The Sheikh didn't move. He stood in front of her, immovable as a granite cliff. His gaze was like a searchlight, the impossible turquoise depths as icy as a glacial lake. 'Did I say you could leave?'

Ivy stiffened. 'No, but—'

'Because if you think I am going to let you walk away with my child, you are very much mistaken, Miss Dean.'

CHAPTER THREE

IVY HAD GONE RIGID, outrage flickering in her coppery eyes, giving them a fascinating, smoky gold tinge. Like the very good Scotch whisky he sometimes allowed himself to indulge in after a particularly difficult operation.

Of course, she wasn't pleased at this development. He didn't expect her to be. But then her feelings in the matter were irrelevant.

She'd chosen to come and find him—a difficult endeavour for many far more experienced than she was, let alone one young and pregnant Englishwoman—and if she thought he wasn't going to be interested then she was wrong.

As he'd stood there listening to her explanation for how she'd ended up as a surrogate for her friend, and he'd watched her hand creep over the little bump of her stomach, he'd been conscious of a strange, almost territorial possessiveness winding through him.

His father had been clear: Nazir was not permitted children. And yes, when he'd been younger he'd resented that, especially since there were already so many rules regarding his behaviour. It was only later, after he'd ruined everything, that he'd understood his father hadn't been just imposing arbitrary rules. It wasn't only a cultural tradition that a royal bastard couldn't sire children, it also made for a better soldier. Emotional ties were weaknesses a commander couldn't afford and it was better to limit them.

So Nazir, having just learned that lesson and painfully, had accepted his fate. Accepted that though there were no strictures on a marriage, he could never have a son or daughter of his own.

He'd decided in the end that marriage wouldn't be for him, either. His father, who'd once been Commander of the Sultan's army, had shown him his path and so he'd followed it, pouring his energy into life as a soldier instead. His father's banishment and his own existence had meant he'd never have a position in Inaris's army. So, after his father's death, Nazir had created his own, building a small but powerful military force that many governments and numerous private interests engaged for 'strategic purposes'.

He had rules, naturally. He wouldn't hire out his force or his own impressive military leadership for coups or for the destabilisation of peaceful countries. He refused to be bought by dictators or those wanting to use his army to hurt innocent civilians, or by criminals wanting to protect their own interests.

He had a strict moral code and expected all his soldiers to follow it.

An 'ethical mercenary', some of the media called him. He didn't care. He funnelled cash back into his army and the rest into Inaris, and even though he had nothing to do with his half-brother the Sultan, or the palace in general, in certain circles he was known as the power behind the throne, much to his half-brother's annoyance.

But Fahad didn't dare touch him. Nazir was too powerful.

However, a child changed things. *His* child, to be exact. His forbidden child...

The unfamiliar thread of possessiveness had tightened as one thing began to become progressively clearer to him. He'd never expected to have children. He'd thought that throw of the dice back in Cambridge had been his one and only contribution to the gene pool. But fate clearly had other plans for him, and since he'd never been a man to overlook an opportunity when one fell straight into his lap, he wouldn't now.

He'd have to think through the implications, obviously, but one thing was clear: she was going to have to stay here.

'What do you mean you're not going to let me leave?' she demanded, fascinating golden sparks glittering in her eyes.

'Surely my meaning is evident.'

'But I—'

'But you what?' He held her gaze. 'You're moderately dehydrated and very sunburned. Your guide has gone. How do you suppose you're going to get back to Mahassa on your own?'

'Well, if you would—'

'Difficult enough for a woman who wasn't pregnant, let alone one who is. And no, I'm not going to give you one of my men to take you back.'

'You could—'

'You're also expecting my child and, since you came here with the express purpose of gauging my interest in fatherhood, I've decided that, yes, I would be interested. But I'm also going to need some time to think about what form that interest might take since it wasn't something I was anticipating.'

'I can't—'

'In the meantime, you'll stay here until I've decided what to do—'

'Let me speak!' The words exploded out of her, the golden sparks in her eyes glittering like a bonfire. Her fine-grained skin was very red from the sunburn and now it turned even redder. She looked furious.

Nazir found the tightening possessiveness turning into something else, something disturbingly raw. He was a soldier. He liked a fight. He liked being challenged, and he liked overcoming said challenge. It was a trait that extended into the bedroom too, which was why he liked strong women, both physically and temperamentally. Especially ones that stood up to him.

He'd had a sense that while Miss Ivy Dean might look delicate, she had a spine of pure steel and he could see that in her now, a force of will that had probably decimated lesser men. A will that no doubt was very used to getting its own way.

You would enjoy matching hers with yours.

Oh, yes, he would. But this was neither the time nor the place, and she was very definitely the wrong woman. Perhaps he'd take care of his urges later, with someone else. He had a few women he could call on for such purposes and they were always very pleased to see him.

He stared at the small fury in front of him, debating whether or not to let the interruption pass, because he certainly wouldn't if she'd been one of his men. Then again, she wasn't one of his men.

No, she's the mother of your child.

The possessiveness wound even tighter, a shifting, raw feeling that he didn't much care for, so he crushed it.

He had no time for such emotions, not when they were the enemy of clear-headed thinking. His own father's choices had been poor ones, but he'd been correct when he'd taught Nazir that a soldier had to divorce himself from his emotions. Following orders required neither thinking nor feeling, only doing. And leading men required only cold intellect. A good leader led with his brain, not his heart, and certainly Nazir had learned the truth of that.

'You can't keep me here,' Ivy said furiously. 'I'm a British citizen. I've registered with the consulate. They know where I am. If anything happens to me they'll come and turn this place inside out!'

Nazir gazed at her dispassionately as she went on at some length, not interrupting her this time because, in the end, she'd run out of words, not to mention breath. And then she'd learn that it didn't matter what she said or what she did, he'd made his decision. He'd given her his order and he would be obeyed.

Eventually she stopped, her pretty mouth finally closing and settling into a hard line.

'I don't believe I threatened you with death, Miss Dean,' Nazir said calmly. 'Or offered you violence. I merely said you were to stay here.'

Her chin lifted. 'Your reputation would say otherwise.'

'But, as you've already ascertained, that reputation is merely a rumour I put around to discourage visitors.'

She looked mulish, making something almost like amusement flicker through him. How strange. He wasn't often amused these days—life as a professional commander of armies wasn't exactly fun-filled—and the expression on Ivy Dean's face was a nice distraction.

She had no apparent fear of him and seemed determined to get her own way, despite being an Englishwoman on her own in a fortress full of elite soldiers, any one of whom could kill her easily should he give the word.

Not that he would. He'd never harmed a woman yet and he wasn't about to start. Still, she didn't appear to understand that if she was going to be afraid of anyone, it should be him. It was almost as if she found him…unimpressive.

Well. That would change.

'I can't stay any longer than a couple of hours,' she warned. 'I'd like to get back to Mahassa before dark.'

She would not be back in Mahassa before dark. He could fly her there in one of his helicopters, of course, but he wasn't going to. Not yet at least. He needed to think through the implications of a few things before he made any definitive decision, and until that happened she would stay here, where he could keep an eye on her and the baby.

'You will stay for exactly as long as I need you to stay.' Automatically, he flicked an impersonal glance over her, the way he would do with any of his men— their well-being was always his top priority since an army was only as strong as its weakest soldier. Her shoulders were set in lines of obvious tension, one hand clenched in a fist at her side while the other rested on her stomach. He'd noticed her do that a couple of times already. Perhaps she wasn't quite as ambivalent about the child as she seemed.

The snaking sense of possession coiled and shifted in response, as if something in him liked that she was protective of the child. *Their* child.

But no, he couldn't afford to start thinking like that. Regardless of what he decided to do about it, the baby was simply an opportunity and he needed to treat it as such.

She looked tired, though, and no wonder; she'd trekked all the way through the desert in the heat of the day to confront him, getting sunburned and dehydrated. It must have taken some courage to do that and then to face him as well. All to fulfil some promise she'd made to a friend.

'You know I won't hurt you,' he said suddenly,

prompted by what urge he wasn't sure. 'You're safe here.'

She blinked and then that stubborn chin came up. 'What? You think I'm afraid? Of you?' Her gaze travelled over him, taking him in, and he was conscious of a certain tightening and a brief flicker of heat right down low inside him. As if some part of him liked the way she looked him over.

Then she sniffed. 'I don't think so.'

Again, amusement caught at him. She was very determined to remain unimpressed by him, wasn't she? Now why was that? In his experience, women had a variety of responses to him, but being unimpressed was not one of them. Not that being impressed by him was something he demanded, but it would have been more convincing if he hadn't noted the flush of colour that had stained her cheeks as she'd stared at him, visible even through her sunburn. Or how her gaze had lingered on his chest where his robe parted.

Interesting. Nazir filed that particular observation away for future reference, since he was not a man to ignore a detail, no matter how insignificant, and it could prove useful at a later date.

'You might come to revise that opinion,' he said casually. 'Besides, regardless of what you think of me, you're tired and need more liquids, and probably some food too.'

'I'm fine. Don't feel you have to put yourself out on my account.'

Nazir ignored her, turning and striding to the door. He pulled it open and issued some orders to the guards standing outside. One headed straight off across the courtyard to the fortress, while the other came obediently into the guardhouse.

'You will go with my guard.' Nazir met her gaze. 'He'll escort you to the library.'

'I'm quite happy here, thank you,' she insisted.

'You'll go where you're told. Stubbornness for the sake of being contrary is not an attractive trait, Miss Dean. I suggest you rethink it.'

More fascinating little sparks of temper glittered in her eyes, but all she said was, 'Very well.'

That lurking heat flickered through him, rousing at the slight hint of challenge in her voice. He ignored it. Whatever he decided to do about Miss Ivy Dean and the child she was carrying—his child—he would make the decision the way he made all his decisions: coldly and cleanly and definitely without any input from other body parts.

You would enjoy taking her, though.

Nazir forced the thought from *that* particular body part away. His own enjoyment was the least of his concerns and he never factored it into any of the decisions he made.

'You're not to venture out into the rest of the fortress,' he added, in case she thought otherwise. 'You'll remain where you're put. Understand?'

She didn't like that; he could see the irritation in her gaze. 'Wasn't I supposed to be safe here?'

'Oh, you are. But I don't trust strangers wandering around like tourists.'

Ivy opened her mouth.

'That's my final word,' Nazir said flatly, before she could speak. 'You would do well to obey me, Miss Dean. You won't like the consequences otherwise.'

Ivy didn't particularly want to follow the guard into the Sheikh's imposing fortress, but she'd been left with little choice. She either went with the guard or…

You won't like the consequences otherwise…

The echo of the Sheikh's deep voice rubbed up against her nerve-endings like sandpaper.

She'd dearly wanted to make a fuss but that comment about being stubborn for the sake of being contrary had hit home, making her realise that he'd been right about that, plus a couple of other things she hadn't wanted him to be right about. Such as the fact that she was still very thirsty and, yes, hungry too. She'd even go so far as to admit that she was also tired.

It was annoying that he'd somehow managed to pick up on those things, especially when she'd been trying very hard not to let even a hint of vulnerability or weakness show. But then he'd told her that she was to stay here, that he couldn't permit her to leave and…well, that had alarmed her. She'd expected he'd need some time to process the news and had thought that she'd go back to Mahassa and wait a few days for him to decide what he wanted to do. Depending on his answer, she'd then catch a flight back to England after that. She didn't want to be away too long because the kids in the home needed her and though the person she'd left in charge in her absence was competent, she didn't care about the details, not like Ivy.

Ignoring the kick of worry, since there was nothing to do be done about it, Ivy followed the guard through the huge double doors of the fortress. Inside it was unexpectedly cool as a result of the insulating effects of thick stone walls and heavy stone floors. The high ceilings too helped. The air was dry, smelling of dust and a strange spice that was oddly pleasant.

The guard's boots echoed on the flagstone floors as he led her down a series of narrow corridors and into a big, featureless room. A few bookcases stood up against the walls and there were a couple of desks and chairs in the middle. It was spartan, utilitarian, and office-like. It was also spotless.

The guard indicated to one of the chairs in invitation, clicked his heels together, then turned and left without so much as a word, shutting the door after him.

Ivy stood a moment, staring around at the austere space. There was nothing soft about it, nothing comforting. There was nowhere to curl up in with a book or even lounge a little. The chairs were bare wood and clearly designed to be used in conjunction with a desk rather than as a place to rest. The one break in all the hard surfaces and uncomfortable angles was a window set into the thick stone walls that looked out onto some unexpected greenery.

Ivy moved over to it and peered out, surprised to catch a glimpse of a lush garden courtyard, providing a cool visual relief from the dust and hot desert sand.

She could even see a fountain playing, the faint sound of it musical despite the thick stone walls.

How strange to find something so beautiful in the middle of a fortress commanded by a notorious desert warlord.

She found her thoughts drifting to the Commander again, to the uncompromising, harsh lines of his face and his astonishing eyes, so clear and so cold. He didn't seem like a man who would enjoy a garden. He didn't seem like a man who enjoyed much of anything at all.

What kind of father would he be? A hard one, that was clear. Stern and very strict. He probably didn't like children—certainly he hadn't been pleased about her news, though that could have been shock. Did she really want a man like him being involved in the upbringing of Connie's child? Perhaps it had been a mistake to come here.

He's still a father, which is more than what you had.

Ivy turned from the window and paced back into the room, disturbed by the track of her own thoughts. Her own situation had nothing to do with this or with him for that matter. What was best for the baby was what counted and if what was best for the baby was to have this hard, stern man in its life then she would have to deal with it.

What if he doesn't want to be in the child's life?

Ice collected in her gut. She'd done her best not to think about that, because she didn't have any answers to that question. Connie had gone downhill very quickly and there had been no time to put in place any back-up plans, not that she had a lot of options. She either put the baby up for adoption or she cared for it herself, and since the thought of putting Connie's baby up for adoption made her feel cold inside, that left only caring for the baby herself.

You? A mother? Are you kidding?

The thought wrapped around her, cold and sharp. It was true that she knew nothing about motherhood or even about being in a family, since she'd had none of her own. The child of a single mother, she'd gone into the foster system at three after her mother had died and had, effectively, never come out of it.

She'd grown up in the children's home she now managed, the only kid who'd never been adopted. That had been tough, but it had worked out well in the end since the home manager had valued her organisational skills and had eventually employed her.

But organisational skills on their own didn't make a good parent. You had to have love for that to happen and her experience of love was non-existent. The children's home had been fine and she'd been well cared for. But she hadn't had anyone care *about* her. She hadn't had anyone love her. So how could she give a child what she herself had never had? She could try, it was true, but what if she got it wrong? What kind of legacy would that be for Connie?

A sharp rap on the door came, then it opened, admitting a woman dressed in a plain black uniform and carrying several trays. The woman nodded to

Ivy, carried the trays to one of the desks, deposited them there and then left without a word.

Ivy stared at what the woman had delivered in amazement.

She'd told the Sheikh that she only required a sandwich and more of that lemonade, but she hadn't expected...this.

There were sandwiches, yes, but not the kind of sandwich she would have expected a soldier to make, or even ones she'd make herself. They were club sandwiches, all of them with different fillings, cut with care and exquisitely arranged on a silver tray, along with a few other delicious-looking savouries. On another tray were arranged some delicate cupcakes, each one a different flavour and all beautifully frosted. A pitcher of lemonade stood next to the cupcakes along with another glass full of ice and a sprig of fresh mint.

Ivy approached the desk where the food sat and frowned suspiciously at it. It looked like something that should be served at a five-star hotel's high tea, not a meal prepared in the desert fortress of a notorious warlord.

Had the Sheikh ordered it? And if he had, who had made it? Because this was clearly the work of a chef who knew what they were doing, not some cook providing basic food for an army, surely?

Ivy wanted to find fault with it so she didn't have to eat it, but she knew that was only because the Sheikh unsettled her and she found his autocratic manner overbearing. Which wasn't a good reason not to drink or to eat, especially when she needed it. And if not for herself then at least for the baby.

So she swallowed her irritation and her pride, reaching out to pick up one of the sandwiches and sniffing experimentally, since there were a number of things she couldn't eat while pregnant. This particular sandwich, though, was cucumber, the fresh scent making her stomach rumble and her mouth water unreasonably, and she'd taken a bite out of it before she was even conscious of doing so. It was delicious and, rather to her own surprise, five minutes later she found she'd eaten not only all the cucumber sandwiches but all the other sandwiches left on the tray as well, not to mention a couple of the cupcakes, which turned out to be light and airy and as utterly delicious as the sandwiches.

She helped herself to the lemonade too, more than a little irritated to find the Sheikh's deep voice running through her head, cautioning her to take small sips. It made her want to down the lot in one go, which of course would be a mistake. Giving in to her temper was always a mistake.

Ignoring it, she made herself sip at the lemonade as she wandered over to the bookshelves, looking at the titles. Most weren't in English and the ones that were were old classics that looked as if they hadn't been read in years. It really was a most unimpressive library.

Finding nothing else of interest, Ivy paced around distractedly. She didn't like to sit still at the best of times, preferring to occupy herself with necessary tasks rather than lounging around, but there wasn't anything to do.

She should probably sit down since she was feeling tired, but, with nothing to do but sit in silence, she didn't like the thought of that. Her phone was in her bag, but since there was no Internet access out here there seemed little point in checking emails or texts.

Moving over to the door, she pulled it open, a part of her mildly surprised to find that she wasn't locked in. The hallway stretched out on either side, long and narrow and dark. Dimly she could hear the sounds of footsteps and voices and the low hum of machinery. The Sheikh had told her to stay put, but how could he expect her to do that when there was nothing to do? Perhaps she could go and find someone and ask them how long the Sheikh was going to be. That wouldn't constitute 'wandering around the fortress like a tourist'. That was going somewhere with purpose. And besides, how could she 'rest' when there wasn't anywhere to rest except for the hard wooden chair?

It's not the chair that's the issue.

Ivy ignored the thought. She didn't want to think about the apprehension that sat inside her, an apprehension that wasn't really about the chair. Or about being on her own in a fortress full of men. Or even about their forbidding, aggravatingly autocratic Commander.

It had far more to do with a presence smaller than any of those and yet far more powerfully affecting. A presence she'd been trying very hard to resist as it wove small tendrils around her heart. She might tell herself all she liked that this was Connie's child and nothing to do with her, but Connie was gone and now this baby had no one but her to look after it. And she *was* afraid. Afraid she would let it down somehow. Afraid that she wouldn't be the kind of mother the child deserved. Not that she wanted to be its mother. Connie should have been its mother.

Connie is dead. There is only you.

Ivy took a breath, her hand creeping unconsciously down over her stomach. This wasn't about being contrary, no matter what the Sheikh had said. This was for Connie and for the baby. She had to find out what was happening and she wasn't going to be able to sit down and rest until she did.

Stepping out into the narrow, dark corridor, Ivy paused to listen a moment. Then she set off down it in the direction of the voices, her heartbeat thudding fast.

'The library is not in that direction, Miss Dean,' someone said from behind her.

Ivy froze, her breath catching as the sound of the Sheikh's deep, harsh voice tumbled over her like an avalanche of rock.

Oh, Lord, where had he come from? She hadn't seen him, hadn't heard him. He'd crept up on her like a ghost.

Ignoring how her heart seemed to thud even harder, Ivy turned to find the narrow hallway behind her almost completely blocked by the Sheikh's large, powerful figure. He was still in that black robe belted loosely around his lean hips, the bronze expanse of his bare chest visible between the edges of the fabric, and apparently her response to it in the guardhouse hadn't been an aberration because she felt the same flood of heat wash through her cheeks as she had back then.

How ridiculous. What on earth was wrong with her? She'd seen a few bare chests in her time, if not in real life then certainly on TV, and none of those had made her blush like this.

She drew herself up as tall as she could, which wasn't very tall and especially not compared to him. The sheer height and breadth of him made the corridor seem even narrower and darker than it already was, and just as impenetrable.

An odd kind of claustrophobia gripped her, her breath stuttering in her throat. His eyes really were the most astonishing colour, caught on the cusp between blue and green, and framed by long, thick, silky-looking black lashes. They were so sharp and so cold, a searchlight sweeping the most private corners of her soul, exposing all her secrets...

'I wasn't going in the direction of the library,' she said, her voice sounding a bit shaky despite her attempts to control it. 'If you could even call that a library. I was trying to find you.'

His expression was like granite. 'You were ordered not to leave.'

Ivy drew her own dusty robes more tightly around her, the sound of her heartbeat loud in her ears. 'You said you didn't want me wandering around like a tourist. Well, I'm not a tourist and I'm not wandering. I wanted to know what was happening.'

'You disobeyed a direct order.'

Temper gathered inside her, burning sullenly, fuelled by weariness and uncertainty and a fear that had been dogging her since Connie had died. Unable to stop herself, she snapped, 'I'm not one of your soldiers, Mr Al Rasul, which means I don't have to obey you.'

If he was angry at her response he gave no sign, his expression remaining stony, and Ivy was seized with the sudden and extremely inappropriate urge to do something really awful, something that would make him angry, something that would make those turquoise eyes glitter with temper and disturb his expressionless mask somehow.

And you used to wonder why no one ever adopted you...

Oh, she knew why. That had become obvious as she'd grown older. She had a temper, a strong will, and hated being told what to do, all of which had been undesirable traits in a child. However, they were more useful as an adult and she'd learned how to harness them to her advantage, especially when it came to protecting the home and the kids she was responsible for.

But unhelpful social workers and government employees were a whole different kettle of fish from granite-faced sheikhs, and if she hadn't understood that fully in the guardhouse she understood it now

as he lifted his gaze from hers, flicking a glance behind her.

'Escort Miss Dean back to the library.' His voice
was as unyielding as iron. 'Then lock the door.'

CHAPTER FOUR

ANGER AND WHAT could only be fear flickered across Ivy Dean's delicate features. It was there in her eyes too, those little veins of gold burning in the copper. But he didn't care.

He couldn't have people disobeying his orders regardless of whether they were his soldiers or not, and definitely not in front of his men. Especially not her. Not now he'd decided what he was going to do about her and the child she carried.

He didn't have to speak—his guards knew what to do—and before the little fury could open her mouth to protest, he'd had them hustle her away down the corridor and back to the library.

It wasn't a comfortable place for her and he knew that. But he didn't have very many places in this part of the fortress that were suitable as waiting rooms for pregnant women. She'd be shown to more suitable quarters soon and, besides, he'd had food and drink brought to her and she'd eaten them quickly enough—or so he'd been told by the soldier who'd been watching the library via a security camera.

Just as he'd informed him when she'd opened the door and stepped into the corridor.

That she wouldn't do as she was told, he'd expected. She'd never be a biddable wife, but a biddable wife wasn't what he wanted anyway. He'd never thought he'd have a wife at all, not until she'd arrived, announcing that she was pregnant with his child, and everything had changed.

It hadn't taken him long to make the decision.

After he'd left the guardhouse, he'd gone to his private office, turning a few ideas over in his head, sorting through the options and implications while she'd been eating the cupcakes he'd had his chef make for her. Yet it had only been when she'd opened that door and stepped into the corridor, blatantly disobeying him, that he'd decided. It was a snap decision and snap decisions were to be viewed with mistrust in the normal scheme of things, but not this time.

He couldn't have her wandering around the fortress, nor could he have her wandering around Inaris. Once word got out—and it would—that she was expecting his child, his enemies would close in. Certainly the Sultan would have something to say about it and once he knew then the danger to both Ivy and the child would increase exponentially.

Even in England they wouldn't be safe. They wouldn't be safe anywhere except here, where he had an entire army to protect them.

So, he couldn't let her go. She and the child would have to stay here with him. And, in order to leave no loopholes by which his enemies could harm her, the child or him, he'd have to marry her.

It wasn't only to protect his child legally; there were other factors involved. Growing up as the product of his father's affair with the Sultan's wife hadn't been easy. His connection to the Sultana had had to remain a secret so as not to risk exposing her to her husband's wrath. The Sultan had been a cold, cruel man and Nazir hadn't blamed his mother for seeking companionship in the arms of another. She'd managed to hide her pregnancy from the Sultan as it had progressed through artful clothing choices and aided by the fact that she didn't show. Eventually she'd gone on a month long 'holiday' to have her baby in secret, accompanied by a trusted maid who was the only other person apart from his father who'd known what was going on. His birth had been a mistake though, and he'd felt the burden of that growing up.

He was a living, breathing reminder of his mother's infidelity, a constant threat to her position. It had been a pressure that he wouldn't wish on any child, especially his own, and, even though the circumstances here were different, he wasn't going to leave anything to chance.

This child would be acknowledged. And he or she would have both parents.

The little fury might have something to say about it, naturally, but her personal feelings on the subject were irrelevant. She'd have to put them aside for the safety of the child, and given that she was also protective of said child—he hadn't missed those little

gestures with her hand—he was certain she'd see
the logic of it.

But several things had to be made ready first, before he informed her of his decision.

Nazir strode back to his office and called an emer-
gency meeting with several of his top aides as well as
the manager of the fortress staff. Various orders were
given. His second-in-command, an ex-Navy SEAL
from California, raised an eyebrow at the announcement, but no one questioned him. No one would dare.
This was a private matter and it concerned no one
else but him.

Once the necessary plans were put in place, Nazir
ordered Ivy to be brought to his office. He'd debated
on how best to tell her, but, since she wasn't likely to
be pleased no matter how he delivered the news, getting straight to the point was the easiest.

She'd also need some time to come to terms with
it, which he would give her, though he wouldn't brook
a refusal, not given what was at stake. Nor could he
let her leave. That would no doubt be a problem for
her, but he wasn't changing his mind.

This was necessary and the sooner she understood
that, the better.

Five minutes later, the door to his office opened
and his guards came in with a very annoyed-looking
Ivy. Her mouth was set in a grim line, her clear gaze
glittering.

Nazir looked her over, impersonal and assessing.
The weariness was more apparent now, dark shadows like bruises beneath her eyes, and she was hold-

ing herself very rigid. This wasn't the best timing for such an announcement, not when she needed rest, but, then again, the quicker he got this over with, the quicker she'd come to accept it.

'Mr Al Rasul,' she began furiously, not waiting for him to speak, her face flushed with annoyance. 'You need to tell me what's happening and you need to tell me now.'

Nazir flicked a glance at his guards, who immediately left the room, closing the door firmly behind them.

'Sit,' he ordered, gesturing at the chair in front of his heavy wooden desk.

Ivy folded her hands in front of her, her chin lifted. 'Thank you, I'll stand.'

Stubborn woman.

He rose to his feet and came around the side of the desk, noting how she stiffened even further the closer he got. It was clear she found his presence uncomfortable, which was interesting.

Leaning back against the desk, he folded his arms. 'You might find it preferable to sit.'

'I've been sitting for the past couple of hours. I do not wish to sit any longer.' Her jaw was tight, her shoulders tense, the agitation pouring off her like a wave.

She needed some direction for all that energy. Whenever he had a soldier similarly agitated, a workout or intense weapons training was a good way for them to expend their nervous tension.

Obviously, though, he couldn't involve Ivy in either a workout or weapons training.

There are other ways to expend nervous tension...

And he would not be involving her in that either, no matter how interested his nether regions might be. He'd marry her, but only as a marriage of convenience. It was going to be hard enough to convince her that she couldn't leave, let alone that she must marry him. Sleeping arrangements would likely be a bridge too far right now.

Heat lingered inside him, though, reminding him of needs that he'd neglected for far too long. Well, he'd remedy that, but perhaps not right now.

'Suit yourself.' He gave her another critical scan. 'You need more food and probably some more liquids, not to mention some rest.'

'No. What I need, Mr Al Rasul, is to be told what's going on.' She enunciated each word as if it were made out of crystal and she didn't want to shatter it.

'I have made a decision about the child,' he said. 'That's what's going on.'

She seemed to stiffen even further. 'And? Spit it out, for God's sake. I need to be back in Mahassa by tonight, because—'

'You will not be going back to Mahassa. Not tonight, and not tomorrow either.'

She blinked. 'Excuse me?'

'You're going to be staying here in the fortress. Where I can protect you and my child.'

Her dark, straight brows arrowed down. 'I'm sorry,

what? What do you mean staying in the fortress? And protection? Protection from what?'

'From *whom*. And as to what I mean about staying in the fortress, that is exactly what I meant. I'm afraid I cannot let you leave.'

'Why ever not?' There was an edge in her tone, the crystal becoming sharper and more cutting.

Nazir studied her, measuring her agitation and the sparks in her gaze. Part of being a good leader was being able to judge the well-being of those he commanded and he'd learned how to read his men. How to tell when he could push them and how far, as well as when not to push. When they needed rest and when they were bored and needed to be challenged. When they were uncertain and needed more confidence, and when they were arrogant and needed to be reminded of their failings.

Miss Ivy Dean was none of those things right now. What she was was tired and at the end of her tether. And perhaps this news would push her over the edge.

He wasn't a man who generally did delicacy or care well, not when he was a soldier at heart. But he could manage it when the situation called for it and clearly the situation called for it now.

'I have many enemies, Miss Dean,' he said. 'And your presence here will have been noted. I do not get many women coming to my gates and certainly not pregnant ones, and so conclusions will be drawn. Correct conclusions, as it turns out.'

She was still frowning. 'So what are you saying?'

'I'm saying that if you return to Mahassa, you

might be in danger from those wanting to use you and the child to get back at me.'

Ivy blinked again. 'You can't be serious.'

'There are many things you don't understand about me,' he said, because he had to and because she had no idea of what she'd innocently walked into. 'But one of those things is that I am dangerous to very many powerful people. Many powerful governments. And if they find out that I have a child…' He didn't finish, but then, he didn't need to.

Comprehension flickered over her face. 'But…why would they…?' She stopped. 'So you *are* a vicious warlord, Mr Al Rasul?'

'That's a conversation for another time. Right now, the most important thing for you to know is that by coming here, you've put yourself and the child in danger. And it's imperative that you remain here in the fortress where I can protect you.'

The angry flush began to drain from her face, making the shadows under her eyes look darker. 'I didn't mean to,' she said, cracks in those crystal tones obvious now. 'I was doing it for Connie's sake. I would never…'

Nazir straightened, beginning to frown himself now, because she was looking very pale indeed and he didn't like it. It was one thing to be concerned for a soldier, but it was another thing again to be concerned for the woman carrying his child.

'Sit down,' he ordered. 'Before you fall down.'

'No.' Her spine went ramrod straight, her gaze narrowing into a shard of copper-gold metal. 'Tell me about this danger. How long do I have to stay here for? Because I have a life in England I need to get back to. And the baby. What about him? And my hotel room in Mahassa? My things are still there, my passport is in the safe. What about the consulate? Surely if I leave Inaris and return to England I'll be safe.'

He waited until she'd finished, conscious of a certain admiration at the sheer stubbornness of her will. She was likely exhausted and in shock and yet was still arguing with him.

'You will not,' he said implacably. 'You will not be safe anywhere but in the fortress. As to the hotel and your things, I've sent someone to retrieve them. They'll be brought back here.'

Her hands moved, nervously smoothing the dusty robes she was still swathed in. 'But how long for? I have leave for another week and then I have to be back in England.'

Nazir stepped away from the desk, moving over to where she stood, still agitatedly pulling at her robes. Without a word, he gripped her upper arms and, with gentle insistence, moved her over to the chair in front of his desk and then pushed her down into it.

Her eyes went wide and she must have indeed been in some amount of shock, because she didn't resist or make any protest, just stared up at him, her gaze full of apprehension and, yes, definitely fear.

The chair had arms and so he put his hands on them, caging her in partly to make sure he had her attention and partly so she couldn't stand up, because once he delivered the next part of his news, she'd definitely need to be sitting down.

Her fine-grained skin was far too pale beneath her sunburn, delicate almost. She was not made for the desert heat, nor was her physical fragility suited to life in his fortress. This English rose would not survive the harsh existence here. Luckily for her, however, he had the equivalent of a greenhouse.

'Miss Dean,' he said clearly and not without a certain amount of gentleness. 'You will have to remain here at the very least until the baby is born. After that, we'll have to negotiate. You said earlier that all children should be wanted and I agree, they should. And I want this child. But if I'm going to claim it then there are a few things you need to understand. My name is a dangerous thing. It is both a risk and a protection. Nevertheless, I want my child to have it and I want the child's mother to have it too.'

Ivy stared blankly at him. 'Your name?'

Nazir could see he was going to have to be a lot clearer.

'I'm going to marry you,' he said. 'And I'm afraid I'm going to have to insist.'

Ivy couldn't understand at first what he was saying. She couldn't understand what was happening, full stop.

First she'd been ordered back into that awful library and the door had been shut behind her then locked. Then she'd had no choice but to sit there for an hour and a half with absolutely nothing to do. She'd paced around initially, fears and apprehensions chasing around in circles in her head, knowing she was winding herself up and yet not being able to stop it.

She hated not being in control of things, hated having important decisions that involved her being decided by other people. It wasn't fair and it wasn't right, and she couldn't do a thing about it.

Luckily, just before she went totally mad with frustration, the guards had come for her, marching her down a number of long, narrow, echoing hallways, until they'd reached a pair of big double doors with yet another guard standing outside them.

The Sheikh's office, apparently.

She'd been shown into a large, but spare room, the same stone floor as everywhere else, and bare stone walls. A huge desk sat at one end of the room, the wall behind it covered in a number of beautifully displayed swords, some in scabbards, some out. There were shelves along the walls, lined with books and boxes and other office paraphernalia, while a large meeting table sat off to one side near a window. This window too looked out onto the strange and beautiful greenery of the courtyard and the moment she'd entered the room she'd wanted to go straight to it and stare out at it.

At least until the man behind the desk had risen to his feet and pinned her where she stood with that icy, sharp gaze of his.

She couldn't go home, he'd told her. She had to stay here. She was in danger and so was the baby.

That had been enough of a shock, but then she'd

found herself propelled into the chair she'd tried to refuse, with him standing in front of her, his hands on the arms of the chair, leaning his massive, muscular body over her, making her feel so very small and fragile and somehow disturbingly feminine.

Then he'd said she had to marry him, which couldn't be true. She didn't know him. He was a stranger and no one married strangers, unless you were on some crazy reality TV show, right?

The definitively masculine lines of his face were hard and set and as expressionless as they had been before, the colour of his eyes startling against his bronze skin and thick, black lashes.

She couldn't stop staring. It really was the most extraordinary shade, with a crystalline quality that hinted at frosts and snows and glaciers. Such cold in the middle of the desert heat. And he was hot; she could feel it radiating from him. It was a warmth that made her want to put her hands out to it like a comforting fire.

Except this fire wasn't comforting and a part of her could sense that. This fire had the potential to blaze and set her alight too if she wasn't careful.

With an effort, Ivy tried to bring her shocked mind back to what was happening. Him. Marriage…

'No,' she forced out. 'That's insane. I can't… I can't marry you. What are you talking about?'

He didn't move. He seemed immovable as a mountain, obdurate as granite, and she had the sense that she could push and push and push at him, but he wouldn't budge. There was no give in him at all.

'You may not refuse.' She felt that harsh voice in her bones, the rumble deep as the shifting of tectonic plates. 'As I said, I insist.'

A burst of shock went through her and she had to struggle hard to mask it. 'But what if I'm married already? What if I have a partner?'

'Are you married? Do you have a partner?'

'No, but—'

'Then that isn't relevant.'

'Why?' she demanded, exhaustion and shock making panic collect in her throat. 'Why do I have to marry you?'

'It will give you some legal protection, especially here, where my name is known.' Something sharp glittered in his eyes. 'Also, the mother of my child should be my wife.'

'But that's…medieval. People don't have to be married these days.'

'I don't care what people do these days,' he said dismissively. 'My child shall have both parents and those parents should be married to each other.'

'We don't love each other. You're a stranger.'

He frowned. 'What has love got to do with it?'

'Only people who love each other get married.' She knew she sounded ridiculous yet was unable to stop. The panic was spreading out inside her and she couldn't seem to force it down and contain it, which wasn't like her at all.

She was normally good in a crisis, she always knew what to do. She was calm and matter-of-fact, and never let her emotions get the better of her. So why she felt as if she were going to pieces now, she had no idea.

Pregnancy hormones, no doubt. Pregnancy hormones and this arrogant bastard of a sheikh.

'I don't know what fairy-tale world you've been living in, Miss Dean, but it isn't this one.' His frown deepened, as if he'd seen something he didn't much like in her expression. 'It isn't a proper marriage I'm insisting on, you do understand that, don't you? Publicly it might look like it, but privately it will only be a legal formality.'

A tension that she hadn't been conscious of released, though she wasn't sure if that left her feeling better or worse.

Better, definitely better. Because why on earth would she be *unhappy* that it wouldn't be a real marriage? It wasn't as if she wanted to sleep with him or anything.

Ignoring the odd flutter that particular thought set off, Ivy said, 'I'm sorry, but that doesn't make me feel any better. Especially considering you're telling me I'm in danger and I now have to stay here until the baby is born.'

'Your feelings on the matter are not important.' He let go of the arms of the chair and straightened, towering over her like the fortress itself. 'The safety and well-being of my child is the only thing of any relevance.'

'He's my child too,' Ivy said without thinking.

One of the Sheikh's black brows shot up. 'I thought *he* was your friend's baby?'

An uprush of sudden heat swamped her, followed by a surge of anger at this man who'd somehow taken control of the situation, making her feel helpless, powerless. As she had all those years ago, the poor little orphan that nobody had wanted to adopt, no matter how good she was. No matter how hard she smiled. So many interviews with lovely potential parents and yet not one of them had ever chosen her. Not one of them had wanted her. And there'd been nothing she could do about it. Absolutely nothing.

Ivy pushed herself to her feet, not realising until far too late that she was standing very close to him, only inches away. And that he was so very tall and so very broad. He dwarfed her. He smelled like the desert, hot and dry, with a tantalising spice that made her heartbeat accelerate and her breath catch.

He was dizzying.

She was trapped by the icy clarity of his gaze and by a strange weakness, as if a tide were receding and she were being carried with it, adrift, and it were drawing her slowly and inexorably out to sea.

Blackness edged her vision and she didn't even realise she was falling until the Sheikh moved, and she felt one hard, muscular arm come around her, catching her and drawing her close against the granite solidity and heat of his body.

She let out a breath, her hands automatically coming up to press against his chest in order to balance herself, yet more shock echoing through her. He felt as if he were made of iron and steel, and yet, as she'd already sensed, there was nothing cold about him.

The hard metal shape of him was sheathed in velvety bronze skin and warm linen, and a very deep part of her wanted to simply close her eyes and rest against him as she would a sun-warmed rock.

His relentless gaze bored into her, his arm hard against her back, trapping her against him, and she couldn't move. She just couldn't move. She'd exhausted all her energy coming out here, confronting him, then being marched into the fortress and having the door locked behind her. And then this bombshell, not being able to leave, the insistence on her marrying him. Claiming the child…

She was so very tired and deep down she was very afraid. Connie was gone, and she desperately wanted to do her best for her friend, for the child she carried, but she wasn't sure she could. And she'd never imagined she would have to do this all on her own…

Anger and grief and fear tangled inside her, knotting together so tightly she couldn't pull them apart. And, much to her horror, the tears came back again, her eyes prickling, her vision swimming.

Oh, God, to nearly faint in front of him…and now she was on the verge of bursting into tears… It was too much.

Ivy closed her eyes and she heard him mutter something that sounded like a curse before she felt herself being swept up into his arms.

She should have fought, should have protested, should have done something to stop him, but she didn't. The last four weeks since Connie had died had just been too hard and she'd come to the end of her strength.

She was dimly aware of being carried out of the office and through dark, echoing stone corridors, the sounds of voices following her, mainly the Sheikh's deep tones as he issued orders.

Perhaps she was being taken back to that library again, which wasn't a pleasant thought, but Ivy couldn't bring herself to care. The man who carried her was very warm and very strong, and it seemed almost natural to relax against his hard chest.

She hadn't been carried like this since she was a child. In fact, come to think of it, had she *ever* been carried like this? Certainly it had been a very long time since she'd had anyone's arms around her, since she'd even been touched. She couldn't remember the last time…

Maybe she'd lie like this for a little while. It wouldn't matter. Just for a couple of moments.

She put her cheek against the linen of his robe, inhaling his dry scent, mixed with that intriguing, masculine spice. She could hear the beat of his heart, steady and strong and sure. It was comforting.

The sounds of doors closing echoed and then the air around her changed, became less arid and more cooling. Brightness pressed against her lids and she would have thought she was outside except there was no suffocating heat. It was quieter too, and calm, and somewhere she could hear a fountain playing.

Then she felt herself being placed on something soft and for a brief second her fingers clutched at him, as if a part of her didn't want him to put her down, but she made herself let go. This brief moment of weakness was coming to an end and now she needed to deal with reality.

Ivy forced her eyes open.

She was in a light, airy room with high ceilings and walls covered in smooth white tiles with a scattering of blue and green here and there. The floors were cool white stone, covered with silken rugs that echoed the blues and greens of the tiles, and a few jewel-bright reds. Deep windows looked out onto a shady colonnade around another, most exquisite little courtyard containing a small fountain and a lot of greenery; she swore she could even hear a bird calling.

There were a few low couches strewn with silk cushions and side tables ready for drinks or snacks or books. Ornate wooden bookcases stood against the walls, the shelves stuffed full, and she could see that many of the titles were in English.

She wasn't sure what kind of room this was, but it looked like the much more comfortable, luxurious cousin of the bare little library she'd just been taken out of.

Shifting slightly, she realised he'd put her down on one of the couches and that it was incredibly comfortable, and, quite frankly, she didn't want to move. The room was cool and soothing and quiet, and all she wanted to do was lie on this couch and maybe go to sleep and forget about the past couple of weeks for a while.

But the Sheikh was crouching next to her, his sharp gaze studying her critically, like a doctor examining a patient and wondering what treatment to give next.

It made her feel exposed and vulnerable, and she was very tempted to close her eyes again, to block him out and pretend he didn't exist. Yet that wasn't going to help her.

He did exist and he was the father of this child. A child he wanted to claim…and apparently her along with it.

She'd never been a coward and so she couldn't opt out now, no matter how badly she wanted to.

'I'm sorry,' she said stiffly. 'I didn't mean to faint like that.' She tried to sit up, only for him to gently push her back down again, his large hands heavy and warm on her shoulders.

'You need to rest.' His dark, harsh voice was full of authority. 'And then you need a shower, some fresh clothes, and more food. You definitely require more water.'

Ivy felt her hackles rising once again, his peremptory tone abrading her raw emotions.

'And no,' he went on before she could speak. 'Don't argue with me. Not only is it a waste of your energy, but you also know that I'm right.'

He was, damn him.

Ivy let out a breath. 'I don't like being told what to do.'

'What a shock.' His expression didn't change and yet she could have sworn his hard mouth relaxed slightly. 'Actually, neither do I. Yet if someone told me to go and eat, and I knew my body needed food, I'd eat, and not waste time arguing about it.'

The strange surge of emotion that had caught her just before was receding, taking with it her anger and her stubborn refusal to give in. She didn't have the energy for it and somehow, here in this calm, cool room, the urgency to do so had faded too.

Irritated, she picked at the hem of her dusty, sandy robe. 'Telling me I'm not allowed to leave and that you're going to marry me didn't help.' She knew she sounded petulant, but right now she didn't care.

'No,' he agreed. 'It probably didn't. But you needed to know my intentions upfront and the sooner I told you, the more time you would have to come to terms with it.'

'You don't have to, you know,' she said. 'I'm sure there are much easier ways to protect me and the baby than marriage.'

'Perhaps.' He rose to his full height in a surprisingly graceful liquid movement then turned, going over to another of the couches and picking up a soft throw in muted blues and greens that had been tossed over the back of it. 'But that is what I've decided.' He came back to where she lay and tucked the soft fabric around her. 'We'll talk about this later. Right now you need some sleep. I don't want you fainting on me again.'

Ivy gave him an indignant look even as she snuggled beneath the throw. 'It wasn't exactly a faint.'

'Swooned, then,' he said, without any discernible change of tone.

She narrowed her gaze suspiciously. Was he teasing her? Surely not. He didn't look like a man who even knew what a tease was. 'Swoon? Do women swoon these days? I certainly don't.'

His expression remained enigmatic. 'You might. Given the right circumstances.'

A delicious lassitude was creeping up on her, as if the warmth and softness of the throw and the soothing sound of the fountain outside were wrapping around her, easing her, relaxing her.

She fought it briefly, determined not to give him the last word. 'And what circumstances are those?'

One side of his mouth lifted in the barest hint of a smile, something glittering in the depths of his eyes that for once wasn't cold. 'Sleep, Miss Dean,' he said.

And much to her annoyance, she found herself doing just that, his almost-smile following her into her dreams.

CHAPTER FIVE

NAZIR FELT ODDLY energised and he wasn't sure why. By rights he shouldn't. The operation he'd just concluded and the broken sleep he'd had before Ivy Dean had turned up on his doorstep should have meant at least a certain level of tiredness.

Yet it wasn't tired he felt as he sat in his office that afternoon, making yet more arrangements in regard to Ivy. He'd directed one of his aides to find out as much as he could about her and then spent a good hour scrolling through the information the aide had sent him on his laptop.

She was an unremarkable woman at first glance, working as the manager of a children's home in London. She had no family, it seemed, had grown up in the home she now managed, and was doing a very good job of it if all the financials were correct.

She spent all her time there, from the looks of things, didn't travel, didn't go out, nor did she seem to have many friends. It was on the surface a small, undistinguished life.

And it didn't match at all the sharp, spiky, fiery woman who'd turned up in his guardhouse.

She was a capable, brave woman certainly, yet one who hadn't thought twice about confronting him or arguing with him. Who'd been afraid and yet had challenged him. Who'd told him she didn't consider the baby hers and yet who'd put her hand over her stomach protectively and seemed convinced it was a boy.

A woman who was very no-nonsense on the surface but who hid a certain...fire.

There were intriguing contrasts to her, he had to admit. She was so sharp and annoyed with him, and yet as her strength had left her earlier and he'd had to catch her before she fell, she hadn't protested. She'd relaxed against him, all warm and soft and delicately feminine. That had surprised him, though he wasn't sure why. Perhaps he'd been expecting her to be as sharp and spiky as her manner, or as flat as her no-nonsense stare. But no. There had been delicious curves and intriguing softness, the gently rounded bump of her stomach pressing against him. And her scent had been a light musk and a subtle, but heady sweetness that reminded him of the jasmine that grew outside the Sultana's rooms at the palace.

He hadn't been sure what had possessed him to pick her up and take her into the part of the fortress that had once, a century ago or more, housed the harem. His father had had it remodelled into rooms for Nazir's mother for their forbidden trysts, and though it was tempting for Nazir himself to bring his lovers there, since that wing was a much more pleasant place to be than the fortress proper, he'd never done so. It hadn't been worth the risk of disclosing the location of the fortress simply for the sake of a night or two's pleasure.

Yet he hadn't thought twice about picking Ivy up and taking her into the bright, pretty little salon that his mother had once delighted in. It had just seemed... right. Besides, there hadn't been anywhere else to take her. There was a set of rooms put aside for medical purposes, but he hadn't wanted to take her there. Everything was austere and utilitarian and not at all comfortable for her.

Her comfort shouldn't have been relevant, just as her feelings shouldn't have been relevant, and yet he'd found himself concerned with both. It was disturbing. He couldn't afford to be distracted by one person, not when he had a whole army to look after and foreign governments to liaise with, not to mention those private interests. And that wasn't even thinking about the Sultan's growing displeasure with him and the private army he commanded. An army that was rapidly growing more powerful than that of Inaris.

His father's life had been ruined by his obsession with the Sultana, his eventual banishment leaving him a broken and embittered man. Nazir would not be the same. Physical passion was one thing, but he'd ensured there was only emptiness where his heart should be.

Once, it had been different. When he'd been a boy, his arid upbringing in his father's house had been transformed by the infrequent meetings he'd had with his mother. He'd lived for those meetings, brief moments of time where he'd had warmth and softness and understanding. Moments when he'd been loved. But they'd never lasted and they'd been never enough.

That had always been his problem. He'd always wanted more. It was a lesson he'd learned eventually, to be content with what he had, but by then it had been too late for his parents. It was his fault, and he knew it. So these days he didn't want anything at all.

So where does that leave you and this marriage? Ready to commit to a life of celibacy, are you?

Nazir leaned back in his chair, frowning at the laptop screen.

His father had been weak when it came to his appetites and Nazir had been contemptuous of his desire for another man's wife, no matter that the only reason Nazir even existed was because of that weakness. Nazir himself would never do the same. He was controlled in everything he did, as was befitting a good leader, and he also put high stock in loyalty.

Still, he wasn't a man who ignored his own bodily needs either. They could play havoc with his ability to do his job and so they needed to be dealt with. His body was a machine and taking care of it allowed it to operate at its optimal level so there was no point in denying it what it needed in order to function.

Which made the question of sex a pertinent one.

If he married Ivy, he was going to have to find a sexual outlet somewhere, and he didn't like the thought of finding it with another woman. He could be discreet; that wasn't a problem. He could make sure that to everyone else it looked as if he were faithful to his wife, but the issue was that *he* would know that he wasn't. And whether Ivy herself cared about that or not—and she probably wouldn't—he did.

He was the product of an extra-marital affair, one that had ended badly for all concerned. An affair that had denied him the mother he could only see in brief snatches of time, where they could never openly display affection, while she lavished all her love on her one and only legitimate son. She hadn't been able to acknowledge Nazir in any way, not without risking the Sultan's wrath, and that had been something that had caused them both immense pain. He wouldn't wish that on any child of his and so any marriage he undertook would have to remain sacrosanct.

You know what that means then, don't you?

Uncharacteristically restless, Nazir shoved back his chair and got up from his desk, pacing over to the window that looked out onto one of the pretty interior courtyards of the fortress that he'd had designed as a rest for the eyes from the desert sands. He found that the greenery and a fountain helped his mind relax, enabling him to think clearly.

Yet for some reason, right now, looking at the green shrubs and trees didn't help. There was a restlessness inside him, a disturbance that seemed to be solely centred on the woman that he'd only known a matter of hours.

Marriage was the only option. He could never not acknowledge his own child, regardless of the danger, not after the way he'd had to be kept a secret himself, and though that acknowledgement was risky to both Ivy and the baby, it would also protect them. He'd thought it would be a marriage of convenience initially, but it would certainly not be convenient for him to remain celibate. And since he couldn't countenance finding lovers outside the marriage, that left him with only one option.

And what about her? What about her feelings on the matter?

Her feelings, as he'd already told her, were irrelevant. However, he'd never forced himself on a woman before and he never would. Yes, his appetites tended towards rough and earthy, and Ivy seemed fragile, but perhaps if she could be persuaded to share his bed, then he could rein himself in. It wouldn't be the best situation, but it would do.

What if she doesn't want you?

Yes, that would be a difficulty. On the other hand, he wasn't sure that was the case. There had been a certain…electricity between them out there in the guardhouse. She hadn't been able to drag her gaze from his and the few times she had, he'd noticed her staring at the portion of his bare chest where his robe had slipped. And then, only a couple of hours ago, when he'd laid her on the couches of the salon, her fingers had tightened on the fabric of his robe as if she hadn't wanted to let him go…

No, there was definite interest there, he was sure of it.

Heat shifted inside him, the echo of the raw, possessive feeling that had crept up on him in the guard-house after she'd told him about the child. He forced it aside. If this had nothing to do with her feelings, then it had even less to do with his.

This was about the child and what was best for it, nothing more.

A knock came at his door.

Nazir turned from the window. 'Enter.'

One of his guards came in and informed him that Ivy's things had arrived from Mahassa, and also that she was awake and had been shown to new quarters.

'Arrange for a meal in the salon in two hours,' he ordered. 'Make sure it's food that she likes and is suitable for a pregnant woman. I will be joining her.'

Exactly two hours later, Nazir strode into the salon.

He'd showered and changed into his usual off-duty wear of a black T-shirt, black combat trousers and soft black desert boots. It was perhaps not quite the right clothing for discussions about marriage or a proposal, but he saw no reason to pretend to be something other than what he was: a soldier, a leader of men. He had a uniform, but he preferred the more comfortable off-duty blacks. It meant he didn't have to change if anything urgent cropped up and they were also much more suited to fighting in.

As he'd ordered, one of the low tables had been set with dinner—freshly made flatbread, olives, hummus, and chicken. A specially prepared salad. Ice-cold water in a large pitcher as well as more of the fresh lemonade. As an added touch, one of his staff had lit candles in small, jewel-coloured glass holders, which scattered flickering light everywhere.

Nazir made a mental note to give his kitchen staff a bonus, then glanced around the room, since it didn't appear to contain the woman all of this had been set out for.

Then, suddenly, a small shape unfolded itself from where it had been crouching near one of the book-cases—a woman in a pair of black stretchy yoga pants and a loose blue T-shirt, a wild skein of long, glossy brown hair caught at the nape of her neck in a loose ponytail. In one hand she held what looked to be a dustpan and in the other a brush.

'Miss Dean,' Nazir growled. 'What the hell are you doing?'

She turned sharply, those amazingly clear copper-coloured eyes meeting his. Now she was out of her dusty white robes and into clothing that was more form-fitting, he could quite clearly see the feminine shape of her. She was beautifully in proportion, with what would probably be an hourglass figure when she wasn't pregnant. Now, though, that figure involved full breasts and a gently rounded little bump that the fabric of her T-shirt clung to.

Nazir found himself staring, transfixed for some inexplicable reason. That little bump was his child. *His...*

'Oh, it's you,' she said, frowning slightly. Candle-light flickered over her hair, which was thick with a slight curl and was the deep, rich brown of chest-nuts. 'As to what I'm doing, I'm dusting the skirting.

It often gets missed and the dust situation near these shelves was atrocious.'

'Dusting the skirting?' he repeated blankly, the words not making any sense to him, not when that raw, possessive feeling was surging back inside him, threatening the cold emptiness that had become part of him.

'This is a lovely room.' Ivy looked around approvingly. 'But there are a few things that could do with a polish. The tiles nearer the floor need to be cleaned and a few of the rugs could do with a beating.'

Nazir blinked, trying to find his usual authority, but it seemed to have vanished. He found himself wanting very much to go over to where she stood, take away her ridiculous dustpan and brush, and run his hands possessively over her rounded stomach and other parts of her, tracing her lovely shape, testing to see whether that delicate pale skin was as silky and soft as it looked. Then perhaps he would taste it, because he was sure it would taste sweet and even though he didn't much like sweet things, he was sure he'd like the taste of her.

And suddenly he was moving, his body responding to the order even as his mind tried to stop him, striding over to where she stood staring at him wide-eyed. And he'd taken first the brush then the dustpan from her hands before she'd had a chance to avoid him.

'What are you doing?' Her voice sounded shocked.

'This,' he said and, dropping the cleaning implements with a clatter, he reached for her.

* * *

The Sheikh's large, warm hands settled on Ivy's hips and before she could move she found herself being drawn relentlessly to him. Shock echoed throughout her entire body.

Now he was out of that black robe, in a close-fitting black T-shirt and black combat trousers, the true power of him was fully revealed and he'd stolen her breath the second she'd turned from her dusting to find him standing behind her.

He was so tall and built like a warrior, all rock-hard muscle and masculine power. The black cotton of his T-shirt stretched over his broad shoulders and chest, making it clear just how physically strong he was, and providing a perfect contrast to the deep bronze of his skin.

He was an intensely dangerous man and she knew it. Felt it deep in her bones. Yet it wasn't a physical danger, she knew that too. No, this man wouldn't hurt her. The danger came from something else. Something she didn't recognise.

Her heartbeat was loud in her head, her mouth dry. His hands on her hips were very warm and he held her quite firmly, the icy blue-green of his eyes glittering as he drew her towards him. There was something…raw in the way he looked at her, something possessive that made her heart beat even faster. And not with fear. She'd never had anyone look at her the way he was looking at her right now. No one ever. As if she belonged to him. As if she were his.

'Mr Al Rasul,' she said thickly, but whether it was a protest or an encouragement she wasn't sure.

He took no notice, his gaze dropping to her stomach. Keeping one hand on her hip to hold her in place, he placed the other palm down on her bump and stroked over the curve of it in an outrageously possessive movement.

Ivy froze. His touch was incredibly gentle and yet the stroke of his hand sent shock waves through her, the heat of his skin burning through the thin material of her T-shirt and into her. She couldn't move. Could hardly breathe.

The last time she had been touched like this had been the light, insubstantial hug that Connie had given her before she'd died. In fact, Connie was the only person who had ever touched her with affection. No one else ever had. No one at the home, no one at school. No one now she was an adult.

The sensation was shocking, setting off a disturbing ache inside her. A hunger that had nothing to do with food.

Her mouth had gone utterly dry. What was she doing just standing there? Letting him touch her as if he had every right to? Because he didn't. He had no right at all. She was a stranger to him and…and…

'Stop,' she said huskily, disturbed to find she was trembling all over.

His gaze caught hers and held it, and in the clear, icy depths of it something hot began to burn. He spread his fingers out possessively on her stomach. 'This is mine.' The deep, harsh timbre of his voice had somehow become even deeper, a raw thread running through it. 'And so are you.'

She stiffened, even as something inside her jolted, a short, sharp electric shock. 'What are you talking about? I'm not yours.'

'Yes, you are.' The light in his eyes glowed hotter, like a glimpse of lava beneath a cold crust of rock. 'You came to me with my child. And that makes you mine.'

Another electric shock zigzagged though her like lightning, a bolt of white heat that felt as if it were shattering her into pieces. It didn't make any sense. She barely knew this man and he certainly didn't know her. Not enough to put a hand on her stomach and tell her that she was his. No one else had ever wanted her, not one single person. She'd been the only child in the home who'd remained unadopted. She'd never had a family. Never had parents who'd loved her and cared for her. Never had siblings to argue with and share with. She'd grown up unwanted, yet she'd made what family she could at the home. Connie, who like her had grown up in the home, though she'd eventually been adopted, had been like a sister to her. Ivy hadn't missed out entirely.

So there was no reason for her to ache like this. To feel so hungry. To want more than just his hand resting there…

Dangerous to want that.

Ivy jerked herself from his grip and took a couple of steps back, putting some space between them. He let her go, making no move towards her, but that possessive light in his eyes didn't fade.

'It seems we have much to discuss.' There was an edge of a growl in his voice. 'Come and eat.'

She didn't want to. That ache, that hunger, was making her wary. It was putting her into a danger that she couldn't see and that wasn't obvious, but that she could feel very strongly. A danger she couldn't put into words. It was similar to the feeling she'd always got as a child whenever she'd had a meeting with potential adoptive parents. When she'd sit there with them, hoping and hoping, desperation radiating from every pore. It was that desperation that put them off, she knew. It repelled people. No one liked a desperate, needy kid. It had been a hard and bitter lesson, but she'd learned it. She'd forced that neediness down, chased it away, and these days she made sure that the last thing she ever did was to need something or someone. She'd found her purpose in helping foster kids instead, in giving them the home she'd never had herself.

But you never quite got rid of the desperation, did you?

Ivy shoved that thought away. She wasn't needy or desperate right now, and she never would be again. And the annoying Sheikh was right about one thing: her feelings weren't what she should be thinking about. She had to think of the child and what was best for them, and, if the danger was truly real, then the best place for this baby was with its father. Which meant she was going to have to ignore her own fears and sit down and talk with him.

It would be fine. She was feeling much better now after the nap she'd had earlier. After she'd woken up, a staff member had shown her to a set of interconnected rooms not far from the salon. They consisted of a bedroom, a bathroom and a little sitting room, all looking out onto the same delightful courtyard that the salon did, and with their own set of French doors that opened out onto the colonnaded walk around the courtyard.

The walls were the same white tile as the salon, the curtains gauzy blue and white linen, and the rooms had the same cool, soothing feel. The bathroom had a vast sunken tiled bath and a huge tiled shower, and there was a shelf with various ornate glass bottles and jars full of oils and salts and soaps.

The rooms were beautiful, luxurious—much more luxurious than Ivy had ever experienced in her entire life and it had vaguely shocked her, especially in comparison to the stark utilitarianism of the rest of the fortress. They almost seemed as if they were part of a different building, a fantasy vision of a Middle Eastern sultan's palace.

Her battered, nondescript black suitcase, sitting on the huge, low bed near the deep windows of the bedroom, had seemed even more nondescript set against all that luxury. A small, mean little suitcase, with its meagre store of clothes.

The staff member who'd showed Ivy around had pulled open a large and ornately carved cedar armoire full of silk robes in a rainbow of colours, indicating that Ivy was to help herself to whatever she wanted to wear. After she'd gone, Ivy had touched the lustrous fabric longingly for a couple of moments, then had firmly closed the doors of the armoire.

She didn't need silk robes or luxury bedding or a huge bath. She'd enjoy the shower then she'd dress in her own clothes, and hopefully then she'd feel more in charge of herself and this whole ridiculous situation.

So she had. She'd gone to the salon to wait for the Sheikh, deciding to grill him about the danger he'd mentioned and how it would affect her and the baby, and how exactly marriage to him was going to work.

She'd been early and, since she didn't like waiting, had informed the staff member who'd come in to deliver the delicious-looking meal that she'd like a dustpan and brush to give some attention to the wall near the bookcases that looked a little dusty. This had been brought to her without comment and so she'd at least had something to do while she waited. And then he'd come...

Ivy found her hand drifting to her stomach again, her fingers brushing against the heat left by his palm, and she had the oddest thought that she wouldn't ever be able to get rid of that heat. It had settled beneath her skin, become part of her.

He caught the movement and his eyes gleamed, and she felt heat rise in her cheeks, as if she'd revealed a secret somehow.

Irritated, Ivy forced her hand away then moved over to the low table where the dinner had been laid out. Floor cushions had been set around it and so she sat, her stomach giving the oddest flutter as the Sheikh did the same with a predator's fluid grace.

Instantly he began putting things on a plate, but when she reached for her own he said in a peremptory tone, 'I will serve you.'

'I can serve myself, thank you very much.'

He ignored her, continuing to put little morsels on the plate. 'Nevertheless, you will allow me.'

Ivy sat up very straight and glared at him. 'I will not.'

'You're a very argumentative woman.' He leaned forward and put the plate down in front of her, then reached for the pitcher of ice water and poured her a glass.

'And you're a very irritating man.' She glanced down at the plate, annoyed to find that she was very hungry. The flatbread smelled delicious, the black olives glossy and fat, the pieces of chicken cooked to perfection.

How aggravating.

Is there any point being aggravated? You'll only end up alienating him and that might not be very good for the baby.

She let out a silent breath. It was true, continuing to argue with him perhaps wasn't the best of ideas. Especially considering she wasn't exactly the powerful one here. She wasn't used to not being in charge or not being in control, but she had no choice about it now, which meant she was just going to have to deal with it and accept that the only thing she had power over was herself.

'Thank you,' she forced herself to say stiffly. 'For the food and for the...rooms you provided. I would have been quite happy with something a little smaller and less luxurious, however. You don't have to put yourself out for me.'

He pushed the glass of water across the table to her. 'I'm not putting myself out. These rooms haven't been used in years, though my staff keep them in good order. Apart from the dust on the skirting, obviously,' he added, dry as the desert beyond the walls of the fortress.

Ivy felt herself blushing yet again. 'There's nothing wrong with wanting to keep things tidy.'

His hard mouth relaxed. 'Indeed not.'

He was amused, which should have annoyed her even further and yet she found that she wasn't annoyed. Instead it felt like a victory, which she didn't understand. She hardly ever made people smile and that had never particularly bothered her before. Yet she was rather pleased with herself that she'd managed to amuse him now.

She looked down at her plate, busying herself with the food so he wouldn't notice, piling up some flatbread with hummus. 'There must be somewhere else you could put me. The bedroom especially looks like it should be used for royalty.'

'You're not mistaken. This fortress was historically one of the Sultan's desert palaces and those rooms used to house the harem.'

A little shiver went down Ivy's spine and it wasn't altogether unpleasant. 'I see.'

He raised one black brow, his gaze enigmatic. 'The term harem refers only to the women's quarters. It doesn't mean a sex club.'

More heat rushed into her cheeks. 'No, of course not. I didn't mean to imply—'

'You didn't imply anything. I'm just clearing up misconceptions, should there be any.' He reached for the pitcher of water and poured himself a glass. 'Those rooms were the Sultana's. Most recently, my mother's.'

Ivy stared. 'Your...mother?'

He shifted on the cushion, one leg bent, his elbow resting negligently on his knee. 'Didn't you know? I'm the previous Sultan's bastard.' His tone was casual and yet there was a sharp glint in his eyes that suggested otherwise.

'Oh,' she said, trying to sound neutral. 'No, I didn't know.'

'My father was Commander of the Inarian army. The Sultan was a cruel and cold man, and my mother was lonely.' Candlelight flickered off the glossy black of his hair and danced over the stark planes and angles of his face. 'She would come out here to spend time away from the palace, and he would often go with her.'

An unwilling curiosity tugged inside her. 'And so, you own the fortress now?'

'The Sultan gave it to my father eventually.' The Sheikh gave a faint smile that now held no amusement whatsoever. 'Though it wasn't a gift. It was a banishment.'

'Why?' Ivy couldn't help asking. 'What did he do?'

'The affair with my mother was discovered.' He still made no move to drink the water he'd poured for himself or to eat. 'To say the Sultan was displeased would be an understatement.'

Ivy's curiosity intensified. 'So what happened—?'

'However, we're not discussing me or my parents,' he interrupted mildly. 'We're discussing you and my child.'

She bit her lip in annoyance. She didn't want to be curious about him in the first place, so why she should find his change of subject irritating, she had no clue. Briefly, she debated pushing him about it, then decided not to. Perhaps later she might ask him, or maybe she would have forgotten about it by then. Either way, it didn't matter, since it wasn't going to have any bearing on what was happening now.

'Very well.' She put down the food she'd been about to eat. 'You can't possibly want to go through with this marriage idea. It's ridiculous.'

He glanced at the food she'd put back on her plate and frowned. 'You need to eat. And while you're eating, I'll tell you what's going to happen.'

'What do you mean you're going to tell me? Weren't we supposed to "discuss" it?'

That hot, possessive glint was back in his gaze. 'Semantics,' he said dismissively. 'The marriage will happen whether you want it to or not, as will you staying here in this fortress. Anything else is up for discussion.'

Ivy bristled, trying to ignore the small thread of panic that was unravelling inside her. 'But I can't stay here. I already told you that I have a job back in England that I—'

'The children's home you manage will be taken care of. I've already placed someone exceptionally qualified to take over and naturally all the funds necessary for the optimal running of the home will be made available.'

She stared at him, panic continuing to unspool inside her.

You're replaced so easily...

'No,' she said. 'No, you can't do that.'

His gaze roved over her, but it wasn't either icy or impersonal the way it had been out in the guardhouse earlier. It was territorial, as if he were an emperor surveying a new land he'd just conquered. 'But I did, Miss Dean. And the person who has been looking after the home for you was very relieved to hear it.'

More emotion was welling up inside her, a thick, hot fury to cover the growing panic. That home had been her life. She'd grown up there, she'd worked there, she'd created as much of a family as she could there.

And you were rejected there over and over again. Why did you ever stay?

Ivy gripped her hands together hard in her lap, her knuckles white. She wanted to reach across the table and punch his arrogant face and then maybe scream at him a little—no, a lot—for interfering. But that wasn't going to help. It would also give away far more than she wanted to reveal to him.

'That home is my life,' she said in a low, furious voice. 'How dare you?'

He didn't look away and she could see the force of his will burning in the depths of his gaze, iron hard, diamond bright. 'Then you have had a very small life, Miss Dean. Perhaps it's time to step outside the bounds of it.'

Fury welled up inside her. At him for how he'd taken charge, casually removing her from the only home she'd ever known. Negligently telling her she was going to have to marry him and then basically imprisoning her here in this godforsaken desert fortress. And all without discussion, as if her own wants and desires didn't matter.

As if she didn't matter.

But you don't matter, do you? You never have.

'Excuse me,' Ivy managed to force out, suddenly desperate to be out of this room and away from him. Away from the temptation to punch his stupid face in. 'I've lost my appetite.'

Then she surged to her feet and stormed out.

CHAPTER SIX

'I'M SORRY, SIR,' the guard said, clearly trying to be diplomatic. 'But she still says no.'

Nazir had returned to the fortress after a couple of days in Mahassa, where he'd had a few meetings with Inaris's top military commanders. The Sultan was *not* happy about Nazir's powerful private army and there had been veiled threats about what would happen if he didn't disband it. The situation had been complicated by the fact that Inaris's government was perfectly happy for Nazir's army to remain since Nazir poured most of his considerable funds back into the country for the people's benefit.

It was also further complicated by the fact that he'd been distracted during the meetings due to one small English fury who'd not been best pleased with his so-called 'interference' in her life and who'd now refused to see him for two days straight.

Nazir dismissed the guard and then, knowing he wasn't going to be able to concentrate, dismissed the two aides he'd been discussing a couple of possible new contracts with too.

Then he stood in his office considering what to do.

He'd already made arrangements for a quick marriage and that would take place in a week or so, which left him not much time in which to convince her to agree to this of her own free will.

Intellectually, he knew that she wasn't one of his men and as such couldn't simply be ordered around, but he'd expected that she'd accept the inevitability of what was going to happen and act accordingly.

Apparently not.

He shouldn't have been so blunt at their dinner. Then again, he was a soldier, and being blunt was all he knew. Plus, he didn't want her arguing with him since arguing only made that intense, possessive feeling inside him worse, and he knew what happened when he let his baser emotions get the better of him.

It had been his jealousy and impulsiveness that had led to his mother's exile from Inaris and had left his father's career in ruins, and that had been a hard lesson to learn. But learn it he had and he couldn't afford to fall back into old patterns again, which meant that while arguing with Ivy might excite the hunter in him, he couldn't allow it to get out of hand. He'd slipped once already when he'd grabbed her in the salon and run his hand over the curve of her stomach where his child lay.

He should have stopped himself, but he hadn't, simply unable to quell the possessive need to touch her. She hadn't pulled away. She'd let him stroke her, the sweet heat of her body warming his palm. Her eyes had gone so wide, the clear copper darkening and turning smoky as he'd run his hand over her. She'd trembled and there had been fear in her gaze. Yet that fear had more to do with her own response to his touch than it had to do with him, he was sure.

An inexperienced woman, clearly. Not his favourite, of course, but inexperience could be overcome. He'd just have to go carefully. In fact, he was going to have to do everything carefully if he wanted to get her to the altar, especially since he didn't much like the idea of forcing her there.

You're going to have to seduce her there then.

Nazir wasn't in the habit of seducing women. They either wanted him or they didn't and if they didn't, he wasn't interested. He'd never once come across a woman he wanted that he couldn't have. He'd never once come across anything he couldn't have, to be fair, or at least not since he'd become an adult. There had been plenty of things he'd wanted as a child that he hadn't got—the softness of a mother's embrace, the warmth of her smile, his hand in hers—so these days he either took what he wanted or he simply didn't want it. It made everything a hell of a lot easier.

But Ivy Dean... She was different. He wanted her and yet she stubbornly refused to do what he said, and normally that would mean he'd lose interest. Yet she was carrying his child and far from losing interest, her refusal only made him want her more.

What a cliché he was.

He paced around his office a bit, going over the issue in his head, trying to get a game plan together. No, he didn't like the idea of forcing her into marriage, since that wouldn't exactly make her receptive to sharing his bed, so it was looking as if seduction was the way to go.

Well, he could do that. He did like a challenge, after all.

Heated anticipation began to coil inside him, an excitement he hadn't felt in far too long. Not a good sign perhaps, but then again, his control was exceptional. And besides, he could allow himself a little excitement surely? He so rarely felt it these days, so why not?

First, though, if he was going to do any seducing, he was going to have to get the little fury to see him, and that would be a challenge. She'd probably hold out indefinitely given what she'd already displayed of her stubborn nature, and he didn't have that kind of time. He'd allowed her a couple of days to sulk so far, but his patience wasn't limitless. Perhaps he'd have to insist.

Nazir made a few more arrangements, issued a few more orders, then strode from his office, making his way to the harem. He had guards on the doors twenty-four-seven, as well as a few more high-tech measures for added safety, and, after a brief conversation with the guards to make sure everything was secure, he let himself into the cool, airy corridors beyond the doors.

The tiled hallways and the sounds of the fountains reminded him of his mother, even though he hadn't been born when she'd been here, as if somehow her presence still lingered...

Maybe he shouldn't have told Ivy about her. Yet there hadn't been any reason *not* to. His parentage wasn't a secret. Everyone in the entire country knew who he was. He wasn't anyone's dirty secret any more. And though his father might have been ashamed of him, Nazir's existence being the embodiment of his father's weakness, he wasn't ashamed. He refused to be. He'd spent his life lurking in the shadows of the palace, always on the outside looking in, watching his half-brother get all the attention from their mother while he got nothing. He'd been raised by a series of nannies hired by his father who had strict rules for how his son should be treated. He was not to be indulged in any way. Emotions were the enemy; self-control was paramount.

Yet he'd always burned hot, even as a child, all those emotions seething beneath his skin, all that love and hate and jealousy and rage. He'd had to learn to contain them, make sure they didn't get out, because that heat had the potential to shatter lives if he wasn't careful. And shatter them he had. Eventually.

He moved into the salon, checking to make sure there weren't any small figures lurking by the skirting, but the room was empty. Then he heard voices filtering through the open French doors that led out onto the colonnade, a woman's light, slightly smoky tones speaking English.

He went out, stepping into the shade of the colonnade that surrounded the little courtyard. In the middle of it where the fountain sat was Ivy, standing beside one of his gardeners and talking as the man pruned one of the graceful jacaranda trees that shaded the fountain. The gardener spoke no English but that didn't seem to concern either Ivy or the gardener, the pair of them somehow communicating through lots of nodding and pointing.

Nazir paused in the shade of one of the colonnade's archways, watching her. She was in the same yoga pants and T-shirt she'd worn the night of their aborted dinner, her hair in that same loose ponytail down her back, the sun glossing the vivid chestnut skein. Her small, pointed face was alight with interest as the gardener indicated the branch he was pruning, running his fingers along it, and giving Ivy an in-depth spiel in Arabic about why this branch had to come off.

Nazir prowled closer, since Ivy hadn't seemed to notice him yet, curious as to how this little scene was going to play out. He hadn't thought she'd be particularly interested in gardening and yet she seemed fascinated by what the gardener was trying to tell her, even though it was clear she didn't have a clue what he was talking about.

The sunburn on her face had faded, leaving her with a golden tan that made her light brown eyes seem more vivid, like new copper pennies, and the no-nonsense, stern expression that had been a fixture whenever he was around had faded. She seemed relaxed and interested and curious, her lovely mouth curving in a ready smile.

A pretty woman, all bright-eyed curiosity and focused interest.

Perhaps she will be like that in bed? In your arms? As you teach her everything there is to know about passion...

His groin tightened, the hot possessiveness that had flooded through him that day he'd met her sweeping through him once again. He wanted to snatch her up and take her away somewhere private, somewhere he wouldn't be disturbed, where he could feast on her at his leisure like a lion with its kill.

At that moment, the gardener noticed him and paled slightly, inclining his head and falling silent, causing Ivy to turn around to see what the problem was.

Her gaze met Nazir's and widened.

'Leave us,' Nazir ordered the gardener, not taking his gaze from Ivy's.

The gardener obediently vanished, leaving the courtyard empty but for Nazir and Ivy, the sound of the fountain cutting through the sudden, electric tension.

Ivy drew herself up, her whole posture stiffening, the delicate lines of her face tensing into severity once again. 'I thought I told your guard not fifteen minutes ago that I didn't want to see you.'

'You did tell him.' Nazir came closer, watching her response as he did so. 'And he told me. I decided it was time you stopped sulking.'

Outrage crossed her face. 'I am *not* sulking.'

'Aren't you?' He stopped not far from her, allowing her a bit of distance at the same time as he debated closing it. 'You stormed out of our discussion without a word and since then have made no effort to communicate what offended you so much or why you're so angry. You haven't even wanted to discuss your current situation.' He gave her a very level look. 'You're being stubborn, Miss Dean. To your detriment.'

She'd gone pink, that luscious mouth of hers in an unforgiving line, all the curiosity and interest he'd seen in her face as she'd talked to the gardener draining away. It made him regret interrupting her.

Alternatively, you could redirect that interest to you.

That was true, he could. In fact, that was exactly what he was going to do.

Ivy glanced away, clearly struggling against her anger. 'I don't want to talk to you.'

'I realise that. However, your choices are becoming more limited by the second and you have no one to blame for that but yourself.'

Her gaze came back to his, glittering bright. 'Choices? What choices? You told me that I had to marry you. Then you locked me in this damn fortress, removed me from my job, ensured that going back home was impossible, and then had the gall, not only to insult the life I've painstakingly built for myself, but destroy it as well.' She strode suddenly up to him, tilting her head back to look straight into his eyes. 'Tell me, Mr Al Rasul, where is my choice in that?'

She was very close. She must have been using some of the bath oils he'd had the bathroom stocked with, because one of them had been jasmine scented and he could smell the sweetness of it now, a heady perfume that rose with the warmth of her skin. Her gaze was brighter, alight not with curiosity this time but challenge, and no small amount of anger.

Oh, she might be stubborn, but she was also passionate. A little tinderbox ready to catch fire at the slightest spark. He'd like to set her alight. He'd like to watch her burn and then stretch out his hands to the flames and let himself catch fire too.

This is dangerous. You should keep your distance.

He should. Yet he couldn't bring himself to move. The T-shirt she wore stretched tight over her full breasts and that little rounded stomach, giving him a perfect view of her luscious, curvy figure. A strand of chestnut hair had come out of her ponytail and lay over her shoulder like a skein of discarded silk. It curled around one breast, making his fingers itch to curl around the soft roundness too, to circle the faint outline of her nipple and make it harden under his touch. To watch her gaze fill with hot sparks, not of anger, but desire.

She was so stubborn and argumentative and prickly, and he wanted to match his will with hers, test her, push her, see how far he could go with her. It had been too long since he'd been with anyone who'd challenged him as determinedly as this woman did.

'There's always choice.' His voice was deeper and rougher than it should have been. 'Even if the choices you have are ones you don't like.'

'Again, what were my choices? Tell me, because I can't see them.'

Oh, challenging him like this was the wrong thing

to do, so very wrong. Especially when he enjoyed it so much. He was a warrior; he liked a fight. He was also a possessive man, a jealous man, too, and his passions ran deep. That was why he had to be so careful. But he couldn't remember why he had to be so careful now, not with her. Not when she was his already.

'Your choices?' He took a step towards her. 'You could, for example, have chosen not to come so close to me.'

She eyed him and sniffed, not alarmed, not yet. But she should be. She definitely should be. 'Oh, really?'

'And you could have chosen not to argue with me.' Nazir took another step, closing what little distance there was between them. 'And you definitely could have chosen not to let me touch you.' He reached for her, settling casual hands on her hips and pulling her close, watching as her gaze widened, her mouth opening in surprise. 'And you probably could have chosen not to let me kiss you, but, since you're not moving, I'm going to assume that you've made your choice, Ivy Dean.'

'Oh, but I—'

He didn't let her finish. He bent his head and took her mouth with his.

Ivy wasn't sure what was happening. Her feet should have been moving and her hands most certainly should have been pressed to his hard chest and pushing hard. Yet her feet remained rooted to the spot and though her hands were on his chest, they weren't pushing.

She wasn't trying to get away from him at all. She was simply standing there, frozen, while his mouth explored hers with a possessive firmness yet gentle delicacy that had her trembling.

She'd never been kissed before, not once. She'd never had a man's hands on her hips, holding her still. Never been so close to him that his heat surrounded her and his scent clouded her senses. But she was now and it was...astonishing.

His lips were hot as a brand and yet softer than she'd thought they'd be, moving on hers lazily, as if he had all the time in the world, tracing her bottom lip with his tongue then nipping gently on her top lip. Sensitising her entire mouth.

She couldn't quite comprehend all the sensations that were pouring through her, so much heat and gentle pressure, and a burgeoning ache that stole her breath. The smell of the desert surrounded her, along with its intense heat, and then there was a spicier, muskier scent too that she found inexplicably delicious.

His body was so big and so powerful, the muscles beneath her hands like granite.

He was kissing her. The Sheikh, the Commander, was kissing her.

Her heartbeat thundered, her breath long gone.

His hands slid from her hips, up and up to cup her face between his palms, tilting her head back and then his tongue was pushing inside her mouth in a long, hot, possessive glide.

A flood of heat rooted her where she stood, electricity arcing through her entire body. He tasted…like hot chocolate and brandy, two things she'd always secretly loved, and it shocked her that a kiss could taste like that. That a man could taste like that.

What are you doing? Why are you letting him kiss you?

Both good questions, but ones she didn't have the answer to, because her brain didn't seem to be functioning. It kept circling around to the feel of his mouth on hers, the pressure of it, the glide of his tongue as he explored and the burning heat of his palms against her cheeks.

What had she been doing before? She couldn't remember. Talking to someone about something. She'd been angry too, but the reasons for that were vague.

Everything was vague except for his hands on her, his mouth on hers, sharp, bright, hot points of contact that felt more real than anything else had in her entire life.

A little sound escaped her and before she knew what she was doing, her fingers had curled into the black cotton of his T-shirt, and she was rising on her toes, pushing against him, wanting more of his taste and his heat, wanting more of his touch, because she felt starving, as if she'd been hungry for days, weeks, no…years. She'd been starving for years, never knowing what it was that she was hungry for, and now here was this man, this unbelievably arrogant, annoying man, showing her exactly what her hunger was for.

Him. She'd been hungry for him.

She touched her tongue to his hesitantly, experimenting, and was rewarded by a deep growling sound that seemed to come from him. His fingers on her cheeks firmed, the kiss becoming deeper, hotter. There was demand in it now, and a possessive edge that thrilled her down to the bone.

He wanted her, didn't he? This powerful Sheikh, with a whole army at his back, wanted her.

The thrill became deeper, wilder. She wanted more of it, more of his taste, more of his touch, and she felt as though she might die if she didn't get it. She pressed herself to him, intoxicated by the feel of his rock-hard body against hers, the iron plane of his chest crushed to her sensitive breasts, something long and thick and hard pressed against the softness between her thighs, where she ached so intensely.

Oh, he wanted her, yes, he did, and she liked that so much. It gave her a power she'd never experienced before in her entire life.

His hands dropped from her cheeks to her hips once more, then curved down over her rear, squeezing her gently, fitting her more closely against the hard ridge of his desire. He took her bottom lip between his teeth and bit down with care, sending white-hot sparks of sensation cascading through her. She shuddered, gripping onto his T-shirt, pushing herself harder against that tantalising ridge because it felt so good. She'd never known pleasure like it.

Are you insane? You barely know him and yet you're letting him kiss you senseless!

Her common sense stirred at the thought, but Ivy ignored it. Common sense seemed so far away and boring right now. She felt cold, as if she'd been shut outside a house in the rain and could see through the windows and catch glimpses of a warm fire in a cosy room. He was that fire. He was that warm room. And she'd been outside all her life. Just once she wanted to go inside and be in the heat.

Except then he pulled away from her, leaving her clutching onto nothing, her mouth feeling full and sensitised, her heartbeat raging, her body aching and her skin tight. And she was cold. Cold again.

'No,' she whispered, barely even conscious of speaking. She reached automatically for him, but he'd stepped back, out of her reach.

There was a fierce, hungry look on his face, the brilliant turquoise of his eyes no longer so icy but blazing with heat.

'Stay where you are,' he ordered, the deep, rough sound of his voice sending yet another thrill echoing through her. 'Unless of course you want to find yourself on your back on that couch in the salon.'

You want that.

Ivy took a breath, the thought winding around her and pulling tight. No. God, no. She didn't want that. This man had not only imprisoned her, he was going to force her to be his wife. He'd made sure she couldn't return to her job *and*, not only that, he'd insulted her. He'd told her that the life she'd built so carefully and painstakingly, the life she was very proud of, was a small one.

It's just his opinion. Why do you care?

A good question and one she'd been asking herself

for the past two days, too angry at him and the situation he'd put her in to want to even see him, let alone discuss it. Sulking, he'd said, and he was right, much as it pained her to admit it. She supposed she had been sulking. But she'd been angry and much of the last couple of days had been spent trying to get rid of it. Anger had never helped her when she'd been desperately wanting to be adopted by someone, and it certainly wasn't going to help her now, when she'd been imprisoned by the world's most annoying Sheikh.

The first day she'd spent pacing around in her set of rooms, fulminating about him, cursing him and his lineage, and feeling very smug when she'd told the guards who'd asked if she would receive him that, no, she most certainly would *not* receive him.

The second day, she'd got bored with pacing, and had started investigating the harem section of the fortress, searching for something to do. The staff didn't speak English, but that hadn't stopped her, and eventually, with lots of pointing and gesturing and miming various actions, she'd managed to get them to give her some cleaning equipment. Then they'd watched her with some amusement as she'd proceeded to give the entire place a thorough dust, sweep and polish. Of course that hadn't taken her all day, only the morning, and afterwards some more guards had arrived, bringing with them a laptop so she could access the Internet, and a phone so she could call the home to let them know where she was.

She'd been angry about that too, determined to find fault with the gesture, mostly because she didn't have any family to inform of her whereabouts and only a few work colleagues who would notice or care. And besides, she didn't want him to be nice to her. She didn't want to let go of her anger, since that would just let the fear in and when it came down to a choice between being angry or afraid, it was anger every time. Fear made a person so passive and Ivy didn't want to be passive.

Dutifully, she'd called the home and spoken to her work colleagues, and, while they'd been grateful to hear from her, all they'd been able to talk about was the ridiculous sum of money that had appeared in the home's bank account, a huge donation from an anonymous benefactor. That had made her angry too.

Eventually, sick of herself, she'd gone out into the courtyard to talk to the gardener, because the shrubs and trees were beautiful and she'd always loved plants, and she'd wanted to know how he managed to keep them looking so good in the middle of the desert.

Then the Sheikh had prowled out from under the colonnaded walk, coming towards her even though she'd told his guards she didn't want to see him, and then he'd kissed her...

The air felt painful on her skin, the sun too bright, and she was hot yet cold at the same time. She didn't know what was happening to her. She'd had no experience of sex, no experience of men, had told herself for years she didn't want any experience either because relationships weren't for her. She was too busy with the home, too busy with her life, too busy, full stop. She hadn't met anyone she'd been attracted to, and, anyway, sex sounded like such a faff. Uncomfortable and awkward and just, no, thank you.

Yet the ache inside her now and the desperate hunger that went along with it belied all those excuses. Because that was what they were. Just excuses. Lies to make herself feel better about the emptiness of her life. An emptiness that Connie had once filled as her friend, and now Connie was gone...

He's right. It's a small life you've led.

Ivy turned abruptly away from his burning gaze, the sound of her heartbeat almost deafening. There were tears in her eyes and she wasn't sure why, but one thing she did know was that she didn't want to cry in front of him. That kiss had ripped her open and she couldn't bear the thought of him seeing what was inside: her desperate loneliness and the intense neediness she tried so hard to conceal.

She brushed past him, heading blindly away, only for long fingers to wrap around her upper arm and jerk her back against his long, hard body.

'Don't you walk away from me,' he growled, his breath warm near her ear. 'I haven't finished and neither have you.'

She trembled, horrified to find herself close to yet another emotional meltdown. 'Please,' she forced out. 'Please, let me go.'

'No,' he said, and before she could move his arms came around her, iron bands holding her against his hot, hard body.

A shudder coursed down her spine, the heat of him

surrounding her, seeping into her, warming all the cold, dark places inside her, making her want more, making her desperate for all the heat he had to give.

She didn't want to give in. Didn't want to cry in his arms, but stupid tears filled her eyes all the same. And that meant there was only one thing left for her to do in order to distract him.

Ivy took a shaking breath and turned in the circle of his arms, tilting her head back to look up into all that blazing turquoise blue. Then she put her hands on his hard chest, went up on her toes, and pressed her mouth to his.

He went very still, every muscle stiffening, and she waited for him to shove her away, because clearly she'd transgressed. And part of her was desperate for the distance, while another part hurt at the anticipated rejection, not wanting him to push her away.

Then he gave another, deep growl, the sound vibrating against her palms, and she was being kissed again, harder and with more demand, his tongue sweeping into her mouth, searching and tasting.

Oh, yes, this was what she wanted. This was what she'd been craving for so many years, a deep and secret craving that she had no words for. But she did now. She knew now.

All this time it had been him.

She didn't want to reveal the depths of her desperation and yet she couldn't stop pressing herself against him, arching into the heat and muscled power of his body, letting him kiss her and trying to kiss him in return. She didn't know how, but she didn't let that stop her, beyond self-consciousness now as she touched her tongue to his, tasting him as he tasted her.

He muttered something in Arabic that she didn't understand, and she thought for one dreadful moment that he was going to push her away again, because he took his mouth from hers. But then his arms were around her and she was being lifted up into them, held tight against his chest as he turned and strode from the courtyard into the cool airiness of the salon.

He moved across the room and over to one of the low couches, putting her onto it, then without a word he followed her down and she found herself pinned beneath one immensely powerful, hot, muscled male body.

His hands were on the cushions on either side of her head, his intense gaze boring down into hers, the heat and weight of him that pressed on her exciting beyond words.

'Well?' His voice was all raw, masculine demand. 'Do you want me, little fury?'

CHAPTER SEVEN

HER EYES HAD gone the most glorious shade of copper-gold and her body beneath his was so small and soft and warm. He had to be careful with her and the roundness where his child lay, but it was so very difficult to remember to be careful. So very difficult when she was beneath him and he could see how passionate she was, so much emotion hidden beneath her spiky, prickly surface. So much hunger, too; he could see that clearly on her face.

He shouldn't have kissed her. That had been a mistake, but he hadn't been able to stop himself and, since she hadn't stopped him either, he'd simply taken it. And she'd tasted glorious, hot and sweet and like everything he'd been forbidden when he was young. Everything he'd forbidden himself as an adult.

So why couldn't he have it now? He'd never had enough warmth, never enough softness. He'd never had enough sweetness, either. He'd denied himself for a long time, not wanting to rouse the deep passions that he knew lay within himself. Passions that were dangerous. Yet he'd had years of experience now at controlling himself, so why shouldn't he let them out? And this woman wasn't someone else's, the way his mother had always been someone else's. This woman was his and his alone.

She was challenging, exciting. He'd thought her fragile and not suited to the desert initially, but maybe he'd been wrong to think that way. She certainly had a will that wasn't fragile, that might even be strong enough to match his own, and right now he couldn't think of a single reason not to take her. Especially when she was clearly as hungry as he was.

She was shaking and breathing very fast, her small hands pressed to his chest. Her eyes were wide and fixed to his, glittering with desire and an obvious desperation that made something catch hard in his chest. That made him wonder where such desperation had come from and why, and who it was that had left her so hungry.

'Yes,' she said huskily. 'I do want you.' Her fingers curled in his T-shirt. 'Please…oh, please…'

Did she know what she was asking for? What she was desperate for? Perhaps she didn't; that kiss of hers had been inexperienced, after all. Not that it mattered, since he'd already decided that he'd have her, and if it hadn't been her kiss that had convinced him, certainly the way she clutched him, begged him, all that desperate hunger in her eyes had.

Someone had neglected her, someone hadn't given her what she needed, and so since he'd laid claim to her, he would. He'd show her exactly what she was so desperate for.

It's not just sex and you know it.

Oh, yes, he was well aware. There was a familiarity to her hunger that made something echo inside his own soul, that made him think of long ago when he'd been a boy, watching his mother hug his half-brother. His half-brother who got all the love and the warmth and the softness, while Nazir got nothing but bare earth and rocks, the long hard marches in the depths of the night and his father's cold, harsh attention.

He knew what it was like to want more than that. To want more and never get it.

Well, he would have it now.

'Do you want me to take you?' he asked roughly, watching the flush sweep up her slender neck and over her delicate features. 'Right here? Right now?'

'Yes…no…' She took a shuddering breath, shifting restlessly beneath him as if she was trying to get even closer, making him curse under his breath as the soft heat between her thighs pressed against his aching shaft. 'I don't know… Oh…' Her fingers spread out on his chest, kneading him like a little cat. 'You're… you're so warm, Mr Al Rasul,' she murmured as if this were the greatest discovery. 'And… I'm so cold.'

The soft words made the constriction in his chest get even tighter. Why was she cold? It made no sense, not with all this heat they were generating between them. And she wasn't cold herself, no, she was like a shard of desert sun, bright, searing and hot. Ready to burn.

He shifted on her, so his weight wasn't crushing her. 'My name is Nazir. Say it.'

'N-Nazir…'

The sound was husky and sweet, making every muscle in his body clench in sudden and intense need.

He bent and brushed his mouth over hers, settling himself more fully between her thighs, pressing the hard length of his sex into all that damp heat. She gasped and arched beneath him, her hips lifting against his, her fingers curling into his T-shirt. He nuzzled her jaw and then kissed his way down her throat, tasting the soft hollow where her pulse beat frantically beneath her silky skin.

She was so responsive, lifting her chin to allow him access, a soft little moan escaping as he pressed his mouth there and then his tongue. He'd never wanted to linger over the taste of a woman's skin, but he could see the appeal now. He could strip her bare, lay her out, lick every sweet inch of her body… Not yet, though. She was restless and desperate, and it was driving the same desperation in him, and he had to be careful. Gentleness wasn't something he was familiar with, but gentleness was what she needed because, after all, she was pregnant and delicate and breakable.

It would be like disarming the mines on one of his father's training operations when he'd been dropped into an old minefield in the south and had to find his way across in order to escape. He'd had to go carefully, watching every footstep, and what he hadn't been able to avoid, he'd had to disarm, manipulating the mechanisms with slow, patient care.

Yes, he could do that with Ivy. Except he didn't want to disarm her. He wanted her to explode.

He bit the side of her neck carefully, making her shudder, then moved on over to the soft swell of her breasts. The fabric of her T-shirt was thin, revealing the rapidly hardening outline of her nipples, and he took one in his mouth, sucking on her through the material. She gave a soft cry, writhing beneath him, the movements of her hips against his aching groin sending sharp bolts of pleasure through him, making him want to hold her down, take her fast and hard.

He ignored the urge. She was a mine, an unexploded bomb, and needed care, not roughness and impatience.

He sucked harder on her at the same time as he pushed a hand down between her thighs, cupping her through the stretchy material of her yoga pants.

She trembled and when his thumb brushed over the sensitive little bud between her legs, she trembled even harder. Lifting his head from her breast, he looked down into her flushed face, watching her response as he slowly brushed his thumb back and forth and then around, giving her the friction she needed, feeling the place where his hand lay get hotter and wetter.

Her eyes fluttered closed, long, silky lashes lying on her rosy cheeks. 'Oh…yes…' The words came out on a sigh. 'Oh… N-Nazir…'

Hot little woman. Desperate little woman. He wanted to give her what she needed. He wanted to be the *only* one who could give her what she needed.

The possessiveness that lay at his heart surged up inside him and he shifted again, ripping away her yoga pants and underwear, baring her for his touch. Then he slid his hand between her thighs once again, his finger stroking over slick, slippery flesh. She cried out, gripping onto his shoulders, twisting under him, and he wanted to kiss her, to taste those cries of pleasure for himself, and yet he wanted to watch her too. He wanted to see what kind of passion he could unleash in her, because there was already so much of it. And he wanted it all for himself.

So he lay there, staring down at her face, his hand moving slowly, exploring her slick heat as she moaned and twisted beneath his touch. There was no shame to her, no hiding, no holding back. She'd abandoned herself utterly to the pleasure and it was the most mesmerising thing he'd ever seen in his entire life.

He ached to have her hands on him, to have her mouth on him, but his control felt thin and tenuous, as if he couldn't quite hold onto it, which might have disturbed him if he'd thought about it. But he didn't think about it. Nothing was more important than her pleasure in this moment, than her hunger and how he would feed it, drive it higher, and then satisfy it in a way that no one else could.

He slipped one careful finger inside her, then another, feeling the tight, wet heat of her body grip him. She gasped, another low moan escaping her, arching up as he slid his fingers deeper. Setting up a gentle slide in and out with one hand, he pushed her T-shirt up with the other, exposing the practical white cotton of her bra. He pulled that aside, baring her breasts, her skin milky, her nipples a pretty dusky pink. Lowering his head, he circled one with his tongue, teasing her and making her gasp before sucking it into his mouth.

Then he worked her with his fingers and his tongue, using the trembling of her body and the soft cries she made as his guide, stoking her pleasure higher and higher.

Ivy clutched at him, writhed beneath him, making the ache in his groin more intense. Making him want to tear the T-shirt from her body, thrust her legs apart and take her roughly and hard. And he would do that. Eventually. For now, though, he'd take his time, he'd be careful with her, stoking her pleasure lazily because it was good to have her beg him. Good to have her pleading. Good to have his name in her mouth as she clutched at him and demanded more.

It was good to have her desperate for him and he wanted to enjoy that for as long as physically possible.

She was such a passionate little thing though and she didn't last as long as he would have liked. He brushed his thumb over the hard bud between her thighs at the same time as he thrust deep with his fingers, and she went suddenly stiff, her whole body arching. A shaken cry escaped her and she convulsed as the orgasm swept over her.

He didn't take his hands away immediately. He stroked her, easing her down until her trembling had begun to fade, then he put his hands on the cushions on either side of her head and looked down into her flushed face.

'I didn't know.' The brilliant copper of her gaze was full of wonder and she stared back as if she'd never seen anything like him before. 'I didn't know it would be like that.'

The tightness in his chest returned and he couldn't place the feeling. It was almost like sympathy, or pity, or regret, he wasn't sure which. Something to do with the wonder on her face and her passionate response, and how it seemed obvious that someone in her life had neglected her and neglected her terribly.

But then, as his research had shown him, she'd grown up in a children's home and had no family. She'd had no one at all except the friend for whom she'd offered to be a surrogate and now that friend was gone.

She's alone, like you.

The tightness wrapped around him and squeezed. Ah, but he wasn't alone, not any more. He commanded men. He had his half-brother dependent on the money he brought him. He had power. He wanted for nothing.

He wasn't the Sultana's neglected bastard any more.

'You're a virgin, aren't you?' He watched her face, enjoying how unguarded she was in this moment. As she had been with the gardener just before, alight with interest and curiosity. He'd wanted her to be that way with him and now she was, and he relished the satisfaction of it.

'You guessed?' A crease appeared between her

brows. 'I suppose it was obvious. But...what gave it away?'

Unexpected amusement coiled inside him. 'A few things.'

'Like what?'

'I'm not really in the mood to have a conversation about that.' He shifted against her, pressing his hard, aching sex against the soft heat between her thighs. 'We're not finished.'

Her eyes went very round. 'Oh...'

She was so pretty and the scent of her body, jasmine and a delicate musk, was making that desire, that powerful possessive drive, almost impossible to restrain.

He leaned down, brushing his mouth over hers in another kiss. 'I'm going to take you, little fury,' he murmured, because he wanted her to be very clear about what was going to happen between them. And what it would mean for her. 'And once I do, you'll be mine. And it'll be for ever, because what's mine stays mine. Do you understand?'

She shivered, a painfully vulnerable expression crossing her face. 'Why? Why do you want me to be yours? You don't even know me. If I weren't pregnant with your child, you wouldn't even have looked twice at me.'

For once there was no anger in her voice, only a painful note that somehow pierced him like an arrow. She was totally genuine; he could see it in her eyes. She really had no idea why he would want her.

It's a valid question. And she's right, you barely know her.

Oh, but he would. And what he did know, what he'd seen in the interactions they'd had already, was that her spirit and her will called to him in a way he hadn't experienced with another woman. Yes, he couldn't deny that the baby had triggered something in him, but it was her who'd deepened that connection. Her and that stubborn spirit of hers that had made him want.

'If you weren't pregnant with my child, you wouldn't be here.' He shifted his hands, cupping her face between them, adjusting his weight so she could feel the pressure of him, the solidity of him surrounding her, yet not be crushed. 'And if you weren't the most stubborn, the most aggravating, the most passionate woman I've ever met, you wouldn't be lying on the couch right now with your legs apart and me on top of you.'

A deep red flush swept over her. 'Don't lie. Don't say things you don't mean.'

'I never say things I don't mean and I never lie.' He curled his fingers into the soft chestnut of her hair, holding her gaze so she could see the truth. 'Why would you think I would?'

His stare was so direct and Ivy felt naked. And not just literally. Somehow his touch and the pleasure he'd given her had stripped all her emotional armour from her too, and she didn't know how to put it back on.

She shouldn't have exposed herself by asking him

why he'd ever want someone like her, as if it mattered, as if she cared in any way what he thought of her.

As if you want him to want you.

Well, she couldn't lie to herself, not now. She did want him to want her, and it was perfectly obvious that he did. She could feel the evidence of that pressing against the tender flesh between her legs, where he'd touched and stroked and brought her to the most incredible climax.

She could feel the echo of it through her body now, in the flashes of pleasure that made her shiver and shake. God, she'd never felt anything like it. All she'd wanted was to get as close to him as she possibly could, have him relieve the intense, maddening ache, and he had. His kiss had blinded her, his touch overwhelming her. Sex had always seemed vaguely messy and a little distasteful to her, certainly nothing worth bothering about, and yet the way the Sheikh— no, Nazir—had run his hands over her, touched her... Well, suffice to say her views on it had changed.

But she didn't like how emotional it had made her, how the simple feel of his fingers twined in her hair, his gaze searching hers as he told her things that couldn't possibly be true, made her eyes fill with tears.

Stubborn and aggravating, he'd called her, and yet those things hadn't sounded like flaws. Passionate didn't sound like a flaw either. No, he'd said them as if they were things he liked, things he thought were desirable, and then looked surprised when she'd accused him of lying. She should never have said that.

Because telling him the truth, that no one had ever wanted her, no one had ever found anything remotely desirable in her so why would he, felt as if it was stripping all the protections from her soul and opening it up for his perusal. And his judgment.

She didn't know why she cared. She didn't know why she cared that he wanted her. None of this should affect her emotionally and yet it did, and she didn't want it to. What she wanted was more of that heat, more of that intense, incredible pleasure, not more discussion.

I'm going to take you... And once I do, you'll be mine. And it will be for ever...

That had scared her; she couldn't deny it. And not because she didn't want to be his, but because she had a terrible feeling that she did. That she might tell herself she'd been quite happy no one had ever adopted her, but the truth was that, in her heart of hearts, she'd always wanted to belong to someone. And it was a constant wound in her soul that no one had ever chosen her.

Except he had. And a part of her wanted to surrender to him, wanted to be his. Yet she knew it wasn't really her that he wanted, but the baby she carried. He didn't feel anything for her but protectiveness because she was pregnant, possessiveness because he was territorial, and lust because he was a man.

None of it was about her.

Did you really think it was?

No, but she didn't want to think about that and she

didn't want to compound her error by answering his question. She didn't want to talk at all.

'No, I don't think you would.' She arched her back, lifting her hips and pressing herself against the long, hard ridge that nudged between her thighs.

He let out a hissing breath, fire catching in his eyes. 'What are you doing?'

The pressure and heat of his hard-muscled body pinning hers down was insanely distracting, and it didn't escape her notice that, while she was half naked, he was still fully dressed. She wanted to touch him the way he'd touched her, explore the contours of that broad chest she'd caught glimpses of the first day she'd met him when he'd turned up in a robe.

'You wanted to take me, so take me.' She twisted in his arms, trying to pull his T-shirt up. 'I don't want to have a discussion about it.'

The fire in his eyes leapt higher, giving her the most delicious thrill. She'd never thought that desire could be powerful, that she could use that power, and that she had it over him. Yet it was clear that she did. The flames burning in his eyes gave it away, as did the tension in his body, and she was suddenly filled with the strangest urge to push him, to exert her power and see what his breaking point would be.

'Little fury,' he said through gritted teeth. 'If you don't stop doing that, I will not be responsible for what might happen.'

'Stop doing what?' She tugged on the cotton, her fingers grazing the hard plane of his stomach. His skin felt smooth and velvety, like oiled silk. 'And you've already told me what's going to happen and I'm fine with it.'

He muttered something that sounded like a curse then grabbed her hands, taking her wrists in an iron grip and pinning them down on either side of her head.

The restraint was strangely exciting, making her want to pull against it and try to escape, but the weight of his body on hers was impossible to shift. And that was exciting too.

'No.' His voice had deepened, an avalanche of jagged rocks. 'Keep still.'

'Why?' She arched her hips, the hard length of his sex rubbing against her soft, damp flesh and striking the most intense sparks of pleasure through her entire body. She couldn't believe that she was feeling hungry for more, not after that last climax, but it seemed as if she was. He was hard everywhere that she was soft and the contrast intrigued and delighted her. She wanted to be overwhelmed by sensation again, to lose herself in heat and the rich, dark spice of his scent. She wanted to lose herself in him.

'Because you're a virgin,' he growled, clearly at the end of his patience. 'I don't want to hurt you.'

Well, sex did hurt the first time—or so Connie had told her, and she'd heard that from other people too. But then afterwards it didn't, so what was the big deal?

'You won't hurt me,' she said impatiently, rocking against him again. 'And I don't care anyway. It's just a first-time thing.'

'As if you would know.' He made another exasperated sound deep in his throat. 'Stop moving, Ivy.'

But the sharp order only excited her further, because she could see how close to the edge he was and it was thrilling. It was she who'd done that to him, wasn't it? Ivy Dean, the girl nobody had wanted, the girl nobody had chosen, was turning this powerful man inside out. And she loved it.

'Make me,' she whispered.

Nazir moved. Pinning her wrists to the cushion above her head, he held them in one hand while, with the other, he reached down and pulled open his trousers. Then she felt the blunt head of his sex slide against the slick folds of hers.

She gasped, twisting in his grip as he teased her with it, leaving her in no doubt about who held the power now. Yet the fact that he had it was no less exciting to her, no less thrilling, because she knew who'd pushed him to this point: she had.

Without any hesitation he pushed inside her, the intensity of his gaze holding hers as she felt her sensitive flesh stretch around him. It hurt, making her catch her breath and shudder in discomfort, but he didn't stop and she didn't ask him to. Then the pain was gone and there was only a feeling of fullness, of completion, and a deep ache that made her tremble.

He said nothing, his relentless gaze pinning her as surely as the press of his sex inside her. The lines of his face were drawn tight, the tension in his body making it obvious that he was holding himself back.

She didn't want him to and the urge to push him

harder, further, filled her again. It was either that or she let herself get overwhelmed by his closeness, by the sheer vulnerability of lying here helpless beneath him. And it wasn't so much about being physically helpless as it was about being emotionally helpless. Because she liked being this close to someone, liked how his heat and strength surrounded her, making her feel safe and protected from all harm. She liked it too much, wanted it too much. And she knew what happened when she wanted things too much...

Ivy tore her gaze from his so he wouldn't see, but then he said, 'Ivy,' in that deep, commanding way, that meant she had no choice but to obey. She glanced back to stare up at him.

He drew his hips back slowly, dragging the long length of him out of her before pushing back in, in a deep lazy glide.

A helpless moan gathered in her throat, the movement sending luscious pleasure spiralling through her veins. She tried to move, wanting more, wanting harder, but he kept her pinned with the weight of his body and a rhythm of deep, slow thrusts with long, lazy withdrawals, making the ache inside her get more and more intense. More and more demanding.

She writhed beneath him, helpless in his grip, helpless against the slowly building pleasure, leaving her with no choice but to surrender to it. So she did, letting it move through her, letting him fill the deep emptiness inside her that she'd always known was there, and yet hadn't fully accepted until now. And she had to accept it. Because now he was here, she could feel how deep that emptiness was, an aching void that he filled up completely with the hard pressure of his body and the hot, dry spice of his scent, the low rumble of his voice, and the relentless push of his sex inside her. It filled her up with pleasure too and cancelled out the loneliness that had settled in her soul, which she thought would never leave her.

Nazir moved faster and harder, yet still with control, and she felt the seams of herself begin to come apart, but she fought it, because she didn't want it to end. She wanted to stay here like this for ever, joined and connected to him, surrounded by him, the loneliness of her life nothing but a faint memory.

But then he adjusted the angle of his thrusts, his shaft rubbing deliciously against the sensitive bud at the apex of her thighs, making her shudder, and her grip on herself began to slip. She couldn't stay like this; the pleasure was too intense, and the knowledge hurt even at the same time as she knew the end of it would be ecstasy.

Then even that thought fractured and disappeared as he shifted again, the movement of his hips turning everything into flame. She shuddered and cried out as the climax hit, the ecstasy of it breaking her into shimmering pieces and tossing her about like glitter thrown into the path of a hurricane She was so lost she wasn't aware as he moved even harder and faster, chasing his own release until the growl of it vibrated deep in his throat and he joined her in the storm.

CHAPTER EIGHT

NAZIR GLANCED AT Ivy as the helicopter flew over the last rocky stretch of desert to the mountains in the north of Inaris. She hadn't said anything since they'd left the fortress, not even when he'd announced that they would be leaving for one of his private residences located at a famous hot spring in the mountains.

Some time away from the fortress to get to know one another was needed, away from all distractions, and he'd already made arrangements. He hadn't expected their sexual encounter in the salon only hours earlier, but that hadn't changed his plans. If anything, it only made them more vital.

Ivy had been subdued afterwards, not saying a word, not even when he'd told her they would be going away for a few days. He'd expected her to make some kind of fiery protest or insist on staying put, but she didn't. She'd simply nodded her head and let him bundle her into the helicopter without speaking.

It concerned him. The sex had been unplanned, which he would have worried about more if it hadn't been expected at some point, certainly given their chemistry. And she'd been a willing participant. No, more than that. She'd been desperate.

If I weren't pregnant with your child, you wouldn't even have looked twice at me...

Something twisted around him and tightened.

She was gazing out of the window at the landscape rolling beneath them, the late afternoon light hitting the curve of her cheek, making her fine-grained skin look as if it were glowing.

He couldn't tell what she was thinking.

She'd been so frantic in his arms, so hungry. A passionate woman who'd been starved of affection. Starved of happiness too, he'd bet. And perhaps that was understandable given her background. He didn't imagine children's homes were easy places to grow up in, no matter how well run they were.

She wanted to be wanted, that was clear, even as she fought her own desires.

You can give that to her.

He was a commander and a hard one at that, and he gave no quarter, not to anyone. After he and his father had been banished from the palace, his father had made it his mission to cut the softness right out of him, and he'd succeeded.

Nazir no longer felt the intense urges of his younger days, the desperate need for his mother's smile. The soft touch of her hand in his hair. The look of love that had crossed her face in the brief moments when he was permitted to have time with her, the only sign of affection she allowed herself to give him.

They had been all too few, those moments. Instances of shining happiness and joy. But that was the problem with happiness. Once you'd known it, all that mattered was getting more of it. More and more, like an addict with a drug, until you weren't sure how you could exist without it.

Better never to have never known it at all, his father had often told him bitterly.

But Nazir had known it. And he'd known softness too, and, though he no longer allowed either of those things in his life these days, he could allow some space for Ivy to have some. It wasn't her fault she'd been brought up in a children's home. It wasn't her fault her friend had died. It wasn't her fault that a trip to the desert to honour her friend's last wish had ended up with her being held in a fortress by the father of the baby she carried.

Certainty settled down inside him. Yes, he would give her what he could; he would give her the affection and passion she so obviously craved. He had no dregs of softness left in him, but he remembered it well enough that he could pretend. And if that failed, then at least they had the passion that had burned bright between them in the salon.

He was careful not to allow himself to think about why her happiness mattered to him. It was a redundant question anyway. It mattered because she would be his wife and, besides, the well-being of any soldier should be a commander's top priority. How else could they perform at their best?

But she isn't one of your soldiers.

Nazir thrust that particular thought away as her

scent wrapped around him, soft jasmine and a delicate, muskier perfume that made his mouth water, that made him remember what it was like to have her beneath him, twisting and writhing, her small hands pulling at his T-shirt, trying to touch his skin.

He was no stranger to power and yet the particular power he'd felt as he'd pushed inside her had felt new to him. She'd looked up at him, her eyes widening in shock and a flicker of pain that had gradually given way to pleasure…and wonder and awe and fascination.

Awe he got from people frequently, along with fear. But never wonder or fascination. As if he were a delicious secret, or a captivating mystery she was impatient to get to the bottom of. And she hadn't seemed to care about how controlled he'd had to be so he wasn't rough with her. In fact, she'd seemed more than keen to incite him further, to push him, to test his control…

Anticipation gathered in his gut, thick and hot, along with a dark, primitive kind of need. He wanted very much to chase her, to take her down as a lion took down a gazelle, bite the back of her neck as he drove himself into her, hard and rough and—

But no. He wasn't going to surrender to those needs. He'd beaten the hungry part of himself into submission and he would never allow it off the leash again.

The helicopter soared over the mountains, some capped with snow. The hot spring and the mountain valley in which it lay were in a beautiful place, gentler than the desert and a much kinder place for her than the harsh sun, intense heat, and a medieval fortress full of soldiers.

'Oh,' Ivy exclaimed softly, her gaze out of the window. 'There's snow.'

With an effort, Nazir brought his attention back to the scenery. 'Yes. The mountains are at a high enough altitude. It's particularly lovely in winter.'

She gave him a fleeting glance. 'Explain why we're going there again?'

'I did,' he said patiently. 'Were you not listening?'

'No.'

There was a tart edge to her voice, which pleased him. Clearly his little fury had come out of her subdued mood. He hoped so. He preferred her fiery, because that at least he knew what to do with.

'So we can have some privacy to discuss a few things in more pleasant surroundings,' he said.

'The courtyard and the salon were perfectly pleasant.'

He watched her face and the guarded lines of it while she stared out of the window instead, retreating back into her no-nonsense armour, and he had the sudden, wicked urge to crack that armour. To shatter it entirely so the warm, vital woman inside it could breathe.

'You know what was perfectly pleasant?' He kept his tone deliberately neutral. 'You screaming my name as you came.'

A fiery blush swept over her cheeks. 'That was a mistake.'

'No, it wasn't,' he disagreed. 'It was most pleasant indeed.'

Ivy flicked him a disdainful glance before looking once more out of the window. 'For you, perhaps.'

Stubborn woman. When was she going to drop that armour and surrender? What was the key that would unlock her?

Ah, but he knew that already. He'd unlocked her in the salon, as she'd lain beneath him panting and desperate. She hadn't been fighting him then. Then, she'd surrendered.

'Are you telling me you didn't enjoy it?' Again, he kept the question neutral, all the while watching her like a hawk. 'Or perhaps you let me believe something that wasn't true?'

Her blush deepened. She let out a soft breath and this time when she turned to look at him, she met his gaze squarely. 'No. I didn't let you believe something that wasn't true.'

'So you enjoyed it, then?' He would have that from her. He would.

'I...' The soft shape of her mouth hardened a second, then relaxed. 'Yes,' she said with all the reluctance of a woman admitting to a painful truth. 'I did enjoy it.'

Intense satisfaction spread out inside him, as if that admission had been everything he'd been waiting for.

'Good.' He held her gaze, letting her see how pleased that had made him. 'Because I intend to do it again...and often.'

Her cheeks had gone a very deep red, but she didn't

look away from him this time. 'And if I don't want you to?'

Well, she wouldn't be Ivy if she agreed to everything he said.

'You don't have to keep fighting, little fury,' he murmured. 'Sometimes you can rest.'

'Don't call me that.'

'I'll stop calling you that when you stop being so furious.'

'I'm not furious.' Yet her hand had clenched in a little fist where it rested on her thigh.

He was filled with the strangest urge to put his hand over hers to soothe her. His mother had done that once, when he'd been young and his father had come to take him away, the brief, stolen moment he'd had with her at an end. He'd protested, too young to heed his father's warning to be quiet, and so his mother had said softly, taking his hand in hers and holding it, 'Don't cry, my darling boy. I'll see you again very soon. Until the next time, hmm?' Then she'd given him a little squeeze, as if transferring some of her warmth into him.

He'd forgotten that. Forgotten how that had comforted him. Perhaps that would also help Ivy. So he lifted his hand and enclosed her small fist in his. She jolted as he touched her, her eyes widening.

'Don't get me wrong,' Nazir said quietly. 'I like it when you fight me. But fighting without purpose will only tire you out and it achieves nothing. Save your energy for the battles that matter.'

She stared at him and for a second the helicopter

was full of a tense, electric energy. 'Does sex not matter, then?'

The question hit him strangely, like a gut punch he hadn't seen coming. Because no, sex had never mattered to him before. It was like eating and sleeping, essential to his physical well-being, but ultimately just a bodily function. And it was on the tip of his tongue to tell her that. Yet somewhere deep inside him, he knew that was a lie.

Sex had never mattered before. But it did now. It mattered with her. And why that was, he had no idea, but he couldn't bring himself to lie and tell her it didn't.

'I always thought it didn't,' he said, 'up until just a few hours ago.'

She frowned. 'Just a few hours ago? But just a few hours ago…' She stopped, realisation dawning. The guarded, almost defiant expression dropped from her face entirely. 'You mean it matters because of…' She trailed off again, as if she couldn't bring herself to complete the sentence.

'Because of you, yes,' he finished for her.

She blinked, long, thick, silky lashes gleaming a deep brown in the sun coming through the windows. 'I don't understand.' Her voice had a husky edge to it. 'Why should I make any difference?'

He could see in her face that the question was genuine.

She'd asked him a very similar question back there in the salon, too, about why he wanted her. As if she'd had no idea about how passionate and beautiful she was.

Maybe she doesn't know. Maybe no one has ever told her.

A tight feeling—a familiarly tight feeling—gathered in his chest and he found himself holding her small hand very firmly and rubbing his thumb back and forth across her soft skin.

'Because you're infuriating, aggravating, stubborn, and intensely passionate,' he said. 'You're also loyal and very courageous and incredibly beautiful.'

She didn't smile. She looked at him as if the words had hurt her.

'You don't believe me, do you?' he asked bluntly.

Her gaze flickered and she looked away, back out of the window once more. 'No one ever thought those things about me before.' The words were so quiet they were almost inaudible. 'Why should you be the first?'

He frowned. 'No one? No one at all?'

She shook her head. 'It's not important.'

'Ivy.' Her name came out in a low growl, letting her know that he was not in any way satisfied with that particular answer.

She sighed and then finally glanced at him again, her expression guarded. 'I was brought up in a children's home, and no one much cares about foster kids, so forgive me for being a little sceptical about compliments.'

He knew her background already from the research he'd done, and he could certainly understand such scepticism. Some of his men had been foster children and he knew that coming from such a background wasn't easy. Yet it wasn't all bad. Some people who came through the foster system managed to find loving and supportive families. Though, perhaps she hadn't?

'It sounds like you had a painful experience,' he said neutrally.

She lifted a shoulder. 'It wasn't as bad as some.'

'Why? What happened?'

She was silent a moment, then carefully she removed her hand from his and resumed her study of the scenery. 'I don't want to talk about it.'

His instinct was to push her, but now wasn't the time and this certainly wasn't the place. It would be better once they were at his residence and settled in. Perhaps after he'd satisfied that desperate hunger of hers, she'd relax her guard, lower her walls.

Ten minutes later, the helicopter banked and then came in to land on the rooftop of his private villa. The house itself was of white stone and built into the side of a mountain, overlooking a pretty valley and its famous hot spring.

The place had long been a holiday retreat for Inarian aristocracy, a little town of the same white stone built near the origin of the spring itself. There was an elegant spa resort catering to tourists and a few restaurants and bars, plus the Sultan's own holiday palace, but Nazir preferred to keep apart from people and so his villa was somewhat removed from the town itself.

It was built around a small waterfall that came

directly from the hot spring, flowing down the bare rock of the mountainside and into a deep pool he'd had constructed especially for the purpose. A number of terraces had been built to take advantage of the views of the valley, but the back of the house where the waterfall and pool were located was completely private.

He didn't often have time to visit and hadn't been here in at least six months, but he'd sent instructions to the people he employed to take care of the house to make the place ready for his arrival, and sure enough the moment they landed the housekeeper appeared, ushering them down the stairs from the helipad and into the cool peace of the main living area.

It was early evening and dinner was being prepared, or so the housekeeper assured him, and would they like any refreshment? Nazir gave her some more instructions, then dismissed her, glancing at Ivy as she moved over to the large double doors that opened out onto one of the terraces.

She was dressed in her yoga pants ensemble yet again and he made a mental note to check if the clothes he'd asked to be bought for her had arrived, since he knew most women liked to wear different things on occasion. Certainly he didn't care what she wore; he wanted to see her in nothing at all, quite frankly.

A silence had fallen, tension drawing tight in the space between them.

Ivy had her back to him, her hair in that loose ponytail down her back, the chestnut strands gleaming in the last of the sun that shone through the windows, illuminating the rich texture. Nazir had crossed the room towards her before he'd even thought it through, reaching out to take that pretty skein of hair in one hand, to run his fingers through the softness of it.

She froze, her breath catching audibly in the sudden silence.

The warm silk of her hair against his skin made the simmering desire, which hadn't subsided one iota since their interlude in the salon, intensify. He eased aside her ponytail and, keeping a grip on it, bent to press his mouth to the sensitive pale skin of her nape.

She trembled, but didn't move, the tension coming off her so fiercely it was an almost physical force.

She wanted him, wanted his touch. Wanted to surrender. Yet she was fighting it. Fighting herself.

Poor little fury. All this resistance must surely be taking it out of her.

Her skin warmed beneath his lips and when he brushed another kiss over the back of her neck, she shivered again.

'Come,' he murmured. 'I'll show you the pool. I think you'll like it.'

'The pool?' Her voice was husky and sounded a little shaken.

'This is a famous spa town, but you don't need to visit the resort. I have my own personal hot spring right here.' He combed his fingers through her hair, easing her back against him. She tensed a moment then, as if giving up some private battle, relaxed.

'I don't know if I want that right now,' she said,

sounding stiff. 'I think I might need some time to myself.'

But they weren't in the helicopter now and he wasn't going to let her retreat yet again.

Gripping her shoulders firmly enough that she couldn't pull away, Nazir turned her gently around to face him, letting her see that she couldn't escape, that he wouldn't allow it. 'What is it, Ivy? Why are you fighting me so very hard?'

A small shudder went through her and he caught a glimpse of that desperation, that hunger that lived inside her, once again. She was trying to hide it, trying not to let him see it. She could sense the predator in him and she didn't want to show weakness.

It was too late of course. He knew now.

'Is it something to do with what you said on the way here?' he asked when she didn't say anything. 'About your time at the children's home?'

Her lashes swept down, veiling her gaze. 'Nazir...'

The sound of his name, offered without any warning, went through him like a sword, clean and bright, and just like that his patience ran out.

Her determination to keep him at a distance ended here. Now.

'Tell me,' he ordered. 'How can I make this better for you if you keep pushing me away?'

Ivy's gaze was wary, the pulse at the base of her throat beating very fast. Then she said with a trace of defiance, 'I told you that I was a foster child, that no one cares about foster children and they didn't. Or at least, they didn't care about me. I was the only one in the home who was never adopted. One by one all the other kids were, including my friend, Connie, but not me. Never me.' A flame of anger and a deep pain burned in her eyes. 'For some I was too quiet. For others I was too loud. I had too many behavioural issues or I was too old. Nothing was ever right about me and nothing I did made any difference. And now you're telling me I'm all these things, things I've never been to anyone else, and I...' She took a trembling breath. 'I can't believe you, I just can't. Because I've been wrong before, Nazir, and you never get over the disappointment. Never.'

His gaze narrowed and for whole seconds but what felt like minutes, she couldn't breathe. She couldn't read the expression that flickered across his granite features. It was something fierce, she knew that, but what it meant she had no idea.

She'd given too much away, hadn't she? She should never have opened her mouth, not when everything she said revealed more of the sharp, jagged pieces of herself that she tried to keep secret. That she didn't want to show anyone, let alone him.

But there was something about him that seemed to draw those things out of her. Something in his deep, authoritative voice and in his sharp, penetrating gaze. In the firm hands he put on her, in the way he wouldn't let her hide, wouldn't let her run. Wouldn't let her no-nonsense, sometimes prickly manner put him off.

He demanded things from her that she'd been certain she'd never give anyone and yet here she was, giving them to him in much the same way as she'd given him her virginity.

He drew passion from her, he drew fire. The same passion and fire that she'd fought down and kept hidden, because it was all part of her desperation. The deep neediness of wanting to be something to someone that she couldn't get rid of no matter how hard she tried. The need to be accepted and loved. To be chosen.

But she'd never been chosen and to think that he might actually choose her...well, she couldn't accept it. Once she'd had some interest shown in her by a lovely couple, who'd made the effort to get to know her. They'd taken her out for a couple of day trips then had taken her back to their house, shown her a room they'd decorated for her. And she'd allowed herself some hope that finally she'd have the family she wanted, only for the adoption to fall through. The couple had changed their minds, she was told. There had been no reason given, but Ivy knew why.

It was her. It was always her. There was something wrong with her.

Her muscles tightened in readiness to pull away, but before she could he let her go and stepped back. His expression was impassive and yet his blue gaze burned hot.

'Let me show you the pool,' he said, and it was not a request.

'But I—'

He said nothing, holding out his hand to her, making it clear that he expected her to take it. And she found herself doing exactly that, the warmth of his fingers closing around hers and the firmness of his grip easing something that had become far too tight inside her.

Without a word, he drew her from the living area and down a hallway, the dark wooden parquet illuminated in the evening light. The walls were pale, and heavy beams of dark wood crossed the ceiling above. A selection of the most beautiful hand-knotted silk rugs had been hung on the walls, giving the place a rich, luxurious feeling without it being suffocating or over the top. She'd never been in a place like it.

The hallway eventually led out onto a stone terrace with the mountain soaring upwards behind it. The terrace ended at a deep, intensely blue pool fed by a gentle waterfall that cascaded down the side of the mountain. The rock gleamed and glittered blue and white and pink from the mineral deposits left by the water, and the flames from braziers that had been lit around the side of the pool made the glitter more intense.

It was the most beautiful place Ivy had ever seen.

Nazir let go of her hand and turned towards the pool. Then, without any fuss, he began to strip off his clothes, casting them onto one of the white linen-covered loungers grouped around the pool.

Ivy blinked, her mouth going dry as the intense, masculine beauty of him was revealed. He was broad, heavily muscled, and powerful. His skin was a deep bronze, the flickering of the braziers outlining the broad planes of his chest and the chiselled ridges of his stomach. His shoulders were wide, his waist lean, his legs long and powerful. He was a perfect physical specimen in peak condition. Here and there, the bronze skin was marred by white scars of different shapes and sizes, and it hit her, almost forcibly, that these were signs of a life of violence. Because of course they were. He was a soldier, wasn't he? He commanded an army.

Once he was naked, he strode to the pool with that athletic predator's grace. A set of stairs led down into the water, but he didn't use them. Instead, he paused at the side of the pool and then dived in, leaving barely a ripple. A second later, he surfaced, pushing his black hair back from his face as he turned towards her. Then he held out his arms, the blue-green flame in his eyes offering a challenge.

It was clear he wanted her to join him.

A streak of heat went through her. It was too tempting to resist and he probably knew that. And really, she should just ignore him. But the needy thing inside her wouldn't let her, and before she was even conscious of it she'd begun to undress, first peeling off her T-shirt and then her bra. She took off her sandals, pushed down her yoga pants and her knickers, and then stepped out of them.

He watched her, the flame in his eyes leaping higher, his attention turning intent, making her mouth even drier and her cheeks feel hot. Resisting the urge to cover herself, she walked to the edge of the pool, hoping it was with the same unselfconscious grace that he had.

He followed her every movement, his expression not so impassive any longer but sharp with open masculine hunger. He liked what he saw of her, that was obvious, and he made no attempt to hide it.

Ivy wished she could dive as he had, but she'd never had swimming lessons. She could float and do dog paddle, but that was about it, so she turned to the stairs that led down into the pool.

Nazir moved suddenly, coming over to the edge where she stood, raising his arms to her. 'No. Come to me, Ivy,' he murmured.

She wasn't sure why he wanted to take her down into the water himself, but, feeling awkward, she lowered herself to sit on the side of the pool and then leaned forward towards him. His hands settled on her hips and suddenly she was weightless, surrounded by deliciously warm water and the hotter, harder feel of his body against hers as he drew her to him.

She took a shaky breath, because she couldn't touch the bottom and there was nothing to hang onto except him. But his arms surrounded her, pulling her tighter against him, urging her legs around his waist, her breasts pressed against his iron-hard chest. Part of her instinctively wanted to push him away, to get some distance, but there was no distance to be had. It thrilled at the same time as it disturbed her.

His gaze held hers and the strangest feeling of security began to move through her. Left with no choice but to allow herself to be held, Ivy relaxed into him.

His skin was slick and warm, and he was so strong. It felt as if he could hold her for ever if he wanted to.

He didn't speak, moving slowly backwards towards the softly falling waterfall that fed the pool.

'Don't worry,' he murmured. 'It's warm.'

Her hands were somehow on his powerful shoulders and she was gripping him tightly. 'I'm not worrying.' She glanced up at the waterfall, the drops of water glittering in the light. 'It's beautiful.'

'Yes,' he agreed. 'It is. And it's been too long since I was here.'

'Why? Are you too busy?'

His hard mouth curved. 'That and the fact that I don't like sitting around doing nothing. This is a retreat and I'm not one for retreats.'

'What do you do, then? Fight wars with that army of yours?'

His lashes were long and thick, glittering with drops of water, the gleam of his eyes beneath them no less intense. 'Are you really interested, little fury, or are you simply making conversation?'

She flushed. 'Perhaps I'm tired of talking about me. And anyway, you said you wanted us to get to know one another.'

'So I did.' He moved closer to the waterfall, the gentle rush of it as it fell down the mountain filling the silence. 'I don't fight wars with my army. It's for protection. For example, sometimes governments hire us to protect polling stations for free elections, or hospitals and medical staff in times of unrest, or other parts of vital infrastructure. Sometimes we're hired by private companies to free people in hostage situations or to protect goods and staff.' He smiled suddenly, bright and dangerous in the last of the evening light. 'I pick and choose what contracts we accept, and I don't allow my men to be used in territorial or border wars. We're peacekeepers, not killers.'

Interested despite herself, Ivy stroked absently over the slick skin of his shoulders as she studied him. 'That sounds all very altruistic for a bunch of men trained specifically to kill other men.'

This time his smile held real amusement. 'You're sceptical, and I suppose you should be. But my beginning was as a soldier in the palace guard and the purpose of a palace guard is to defend, not to attack.'

Well, she hadn't known that. 'Oh, so you wanted a military career? Following in your father's footsteps?'

'Yes. There was never any other choice for me. As you know, I was sent to Cambridge for a few years, but apart from that, it was always expected that I would be a soldier.'

She studied him, curious. 'So why Cambridge?'

The light from the braziers gleamed over his sleek black hair and caught at the glints in his eyes. 'For a decent education.' An undercurrent of bitterness tinged the words.

Ivy frowned. 'Why do I get that feeling that's not all there was to it?'

'Because that wasn't the only reason why I was sent away.'

'What else was there, then?'

'My mother.' He moved closer to the waterfall, the

sound of it splashing into the pool musical and soothing. 'She was the Sultana and she had me in secret.
I was brought up by my father. Every so often I was
allowed to meet her and my father would take me to
her so we could spend time together. She couldn't be
seen to be spending too much time with the Commander's child, though, or else people would talk. It
was never enough. Always, I wanted more.'

His voice was very neutral, but she could detect
undercurrents in it, deep and strong. What they meant
she wasn't sure, but she was certain she heard anger.
His expression, however, gave her no clue. His features were set in granite lines as per usual.

No, he was angry, she could feel it in him, and she
understood why. Because she too had wanted more
and never had it. She'd wanted a mother and father,
siblings, a family.

He at least had known his parents, unlike her. Then
again, had he really had his mother? It was clear he
didn't think so. What was worse? To have had a parent you only saw from afar and interacted with in-
frequently, or never to have had that parent at all?

She didn't know. But it made her think of the child
growing inside her, of how at least that child would
have both a mother and a father in its life. Even if that
mother had no idea what she was doing.

He was right to keep you here.

The taut, aching feeling inside her eased, as if giving up a fight, making her lean forward, wrapping
her arms around his neck, revelling in the feel of his
slick, warm skin against hers.

'Tell me about the more you wanted,' she said quietly.

His face was very close, the sunset throwing golden light across the stark planes and angles, his eyes glittering in icy contrast to the warmth of the water and the heat of his body. An intense light burned in them, so fierce her breath caught.

'I wanted everything.' The deep sound of his voice vibrated against her. 'I wanted to be her son openly, proudly. I wanted what she gave my half-brother: her time and attention, her softness and gentleness, her love.' The light in his eyes turned bright and jagged. 'But my father was concerned that I was spending too much time with her. It was fine when I was a child, since it was well known that the Sultana loved children and her attention to me could be explained away. But not when I got older. So my father decided it would be better if I went away for a time. That's why I was sent to Cambridge.'

She'd been right; he *was* angry. Ferociously so. And underneath that anger she could hear the longing for the love and attention he'd desperately wanted and never had. She knew all about that kind of longing. She knew it well.

'You didn't want to go?' she asked.

'No.' His hands cupped her bottom, holding her against him, his fingers digging into her flesh. 'But I had no choice. The three years in England gave me time to think, time to obsess over what I didn't have and what I wanted. My mother loved me and she loved my father, and she was unhappy with the Sul-

tan, and I couldn't see why she had to stay in a life
that made her so miserable. So when I returned to Inaris, I went to see her immediately. I told her that she
and my father should leave, that I would help, that we
could all get out of the country, be a family together,
be happy.' His gaze iced over. 'But she refused. She
wouldn't leave her husband and she wouldn't leave
my half-brother. I was furious, ranting and shouting, and the next thing I knew the room was full of
soldiers. Fahad, my half-brother, had been listening
and had heard everything. He discovered our secret.'

Ivy's heart caught hard. 'Oh, Nazir...'

'There was a confrontation and I attacked him.
My mother tried to stop me, but I didn't listen. I was
too angry, too jealous. He had everything that I'd always wanted, and my mother wouldn't leave him.'
Nazir's mouth hardened. 'But you don't attack the heir
without consequences and I was imprisoned, pend-
ing execution. My mother pleaded for my life with
the Sultan and I don't know what she said, but eventually she secured my release.'

Ivy stared at him, caught by the ice in his eyes in
comparison to the determinedly neutral expression
on his face.

'What happened afterwards?' she asked, part of
her not wanting to know because, whatever it was,
she knew it wouldn't have been good.

'My father and I were banished from the palace.
The Sultan wanted to execute him, but he was too
powerful. Instead, he lost his position as Commander
and neither of us ever saw my mother again.'

A soundless breath of shock escaped her. 'No.'

'For a long time, neither my father nor I knew what had happened to her. She disappeared from public life and there were rumours the Sultan had had her killed because of her affair.' A bleak light entered his eyes. 'My father never forgave me for what happened. I'd always been his secret shame and then I was the cause of so much pain for the woman he loved... I should have been satisfied with what I had.' Nazir paused, his gaze focusing on her very suddenly. 'And that is quite enough about me.'

Before Ivy knew what was happening, he'd taken her under the waterfall, warm water falling down around them, soaking her hair, soaking her bare shoulders, blinding her.

She opened her mouth on a gasp, but his lips covered hers, taking the sound from her, the taste of him joining the mineral flavour of the water, surrounding her in warmth. Warmth from the gentle fall of water, warmth from his mouth on hers, his kiss deep and slow and sweet. Warmth from the hard, powerful body she was clinging to.

She had so many questions, her brain still trying to process everything he'd said, her heart aching for him and what he'd lost, but her thinking processes had slowed, the hunger of her body beginning to take over.

One of his hands slid up her spine to cup the back of her head, holding her in place as his tongue pushed deep into her mouth, exploring her in slow, leisurely strokes.

And it suddenly became very clear to her what he was looking for and what he wanted and what he was trying to create by keeping her here. Whether he knew it or not, he wanted a family. He wanted what he'd longed for all those years ago and what he'd lost in the end.

So why not give it to him? There wasn't any reason not to. They were both looking for the same things, it seemed, and both of them had finally found them together, so why bother fighting? He'd told her that she was his, so why not accept it? Give into it? After all, no one else had ever claimed her. It might as well be him.

The decision settled down inside her and she gripped his shoulders hard, tightening her legs around him, because as much as he claimed her, she would also claim him. So she kissed him back, hungrier now, the water falling on her, the slick feel of his skin, the rapidly growing hardness of his shaft between her thighs providing her with the most delicious erotic contrasts.

But he would not be hurried and he ignored her growing need. He kept his kiss deep and lazy, his fingers on the back of her head angling her so he could explore her deeper. Hunger grew sharp teeth, but this time she didn't feel as desperate.

The falling water soothed her, as did the warmth of the pool, the strength of him holding her up, the slow-burning, lazy kiss, and the decision she'd made to accept what he'd offered her. And gradually, the hunger became less frantic.

The tension eased from her and she relaxed into the slow eroticism of the kiss, returning it with the same tender sweetness.

There was too much water in her eyes so she kept them closed, focusing instead on his hot mouth and the leisurely way he kissed her. He was hard, and when he adjusted his grip, lifting her slightly, the head of his shaft pressing against her exquisitely sensitive flesh, she wriggled to take him. But he teased her for a few moments, making her shudder, before taking her hips in a firm grip and then easing her down onto him, again, so slowly it drew a groan from her.

'Take me, little fury,' he whispered against her mouth, his voice so deep, cutting through the sound of the water rushing over them. 'Because all those people who didn't want you were fools. *I* want you. So give me your passion. I want it all.'

She thought he'd forgotten about what she'd told him earlier. But it seemed he hadn't, and it made something in her heart slip then catch like a puzzle piece sliding into place in a jigsaw.

She wanted to give him that passion because he was a hard man who'd held her with gentleness. A leader of armies who had a courtyard full of greenery and fountains in the middle of an unforgiving fortress in the desert. A man for whom pleasure seemed to be a foreign concept and yet who had a holiday villa with a hot pool, which he never visited because he didn't like sitting around. A vicious warlord by his own admission, yet who'd seen to her comfort.

There were so many fascinating contrasts within

him. It was as if there were things he wanted but wouldn't let himself have, perhaps as a punishment or a lesson for what had happened to him all those years ago. The mother who'd been banished and the father whose life had been ruined by his actions. The family he'd destroyed.

He still wanted that family though, and that longing was so familiar to her. She knew it as she knew her own heart. So she didn't think twice as she wrapped her arms around his neck and tightened her legs around his waist, moving on him, giving him back all the passion contained inside her, until the ecstasy of it drowned both of them.

CHAPTER NINE

NAZIR HADN'T EXPECTED to tell Ivy everything that had happened with his mother. He'd meant to answer her question about why he'd been sent to Cambridge then carry her under the waterfall and kiss that sweet mouth of hers.

But there had been something in the way she'd wrapped her arms around him, something in the feel of her silky bare skin against his, the slight crease between her brows and the steadfast look in her coppery eyes.

And he'd found himself saying much more than he'd intended. More than he'd ever told anyone. He hadn't expected to let the longing he'd always felt come to the surface, nor the anger that came along with it. The anger and jealousy and sorrow he'd thought he'd got rid of years ago, and beneath that a shame he'd never accepted.

Which wasn't a good thing. He couldn't let those emotions cloud his thinking the way they had all those years ago, not with what was at stake. Ivy and his child had to be protected at all costs, and most especially from him.

His loss of control had destroyed the family he'd almost had and his mother...

Eventually he'd found out what had happened to her. After her affair had been discovered, the Sultan had banished her from the country for the rest of her life. She'd died in Switzerland, never to see either of her sons or the man she loved ever again.

That was his fault. If he hadn't lost his temper, if he hadn't attacked Fahad, then everything might have been different. But he had, and there was nothing he could do to change that or what had happened to his mother. The only thing he could do was stay in command of himself and ensure nothing like that ever happened again.

It was an easy enough task, especially when, over the course of the next few days, Ivy stopped being stubborn and challenging. She stopped fighting him, stopped protesting. Her no-nonsense armour was nowhere to be seen, letting the woman she was underneath bloom like a flower in the sun.

And what a woman she was. Warm and vital and interested. Caring and curious.

Like himself, she wasn't much for lying around, and so he took her on a few gentle horseback rides along some of the mountain trails, showing her the pretty valleys and views that could be had from the higher outlooks. He taught her how to swim in the warm water of the hot springs and then, afterwards, taught her how to pleasure him even at the same time as he explored all the ways to pleasure her.

They had meals by candlelight on the terraces and by the pool, and once or twice in some of the prettier valleys near his residence, where they discussed various subjects, including how a marriage would work between them, how and where they would raise the child together.

Ivy had no trouble disagreeing with him on a few points, but it was soon clear that they both believed very strongly that the child needed both parents and a safe, secure base in which to grow up.

'And what about me?' Ivy asked as they sat by the pool one night, the braziers lit, sending flickering light over the waterfall that fell into it. 'I need more to my life than raising a child. Not that that isn't a vitally important job, but I need something else.'

Nazir glanced over the low table to where Ivy sat cross-legged on a cushion opposite him. Her hair was loose tonight, the way he preferred it, tumbling over her shoulders in a wild, gleaming fall of chestnut. All she wore was a light, diaphanous robe of deep red silk embroidered with gold that he'd ordered especially for her. It was a rich, beautiful fabric that made her pale skin glow and brought colour to her pretty face. The metallic thread made her eyes seem even more coppery in the light and, as an added bonus, it was a little transparent, allowing him to catch glimpses of the glory that was her naked body.

At first she'd been uncomfortable wearing it with nothing on underneath, but once he'd shown her how much it pleased him to see her wearing it, she'd relaxed, and now she didn't even seem to think twice about it.

Looking at her and how beautiful and sensual she was, the robe curving over the slight roundness of her stomach where his child lay, made his possessiveness flex and tighten. As if he wanted to fight anyone who came near her, anyone who dared even look at her. And if anyone else ever touched her...

He forced himself to look away, struggling to get control of the hot thread of fury that wound through him at the thought.

She is dangerous to you. She makes you feel too much.

No, that was foolish. His control over his emotions was flawless.

Nazir picked up his wine glass and took a sip of the rich red wine, forcing his recalcitrant attention back to her question.

She did need more to her life and the more time he spent with her, the more that was obvious. He'd told her when they first met that her life so far had been a small one, and while he hadn't meant it to be cruel, he still believed that.

She was exceedingly intelligent and interested and had a big-picture focus that the commander in him recognised as a valuable skill.

There were many organisation systems he had in place that he knew could use an overhaul and Ivy would be perfect for the job. Because in very many ways, she was a commander too. Hadn't that been her role in the home she'd managed? It wasn't an army, but it was people and, in the end, that was what an army was, just people operating within a system.

'I agree,' he said. 'You do need something more. So what would you like to do?'

A tiny crease appeared between her brows as she picked up the tall glass full of the orange juice she liked. 'You know, I hadn't really thought. Back in England I didn't have a lot of options and so I—'

'You always had options,' he interrupted gently. 'You're intelligent, interested, empathetic and full of energy. You would have been a huge asset to any employer or university or training institute.' He paused, watching her face. 'Why did you stay at the home? You could have gone anywhere, done anything. But you didn't.'

She coloured, looking down at her glass as if finding its contents fascinating. 'I had no experience at anything else but looking after the home. And I wanted to make sure everyone in it was looked after and cared for. And Connie lived nearby. And... I suppose it was all I knew.'

He could understand that, just as he understood that it wasn't any of those things that had held her back, not this stubborn, determined woman. She'd crossed a desert, braved those rumours he'd put around about himself and all to fulfil her dying friend's last wish. If she'd wanted to leave the home, she would have.

'You didn't want to do anything else? You didn't have dreams of a better life? Of having more?'

'No,' she said quietly, not looking up. 'It was easier not to. Easier to accept what I had than to hope for something I had no chance of getting.'

The way you've accepted your life and what you have. The way you keep telling yourself that you don't want more.

No, this wasn't the same. He'd been brought up to be a soldier, that was all he'd known, and he was happy with that. The need to protect and defend was part of him; it was in his blood. And so, after his father's death, because he hadn't been welcome back in the palace, he'd built himself an army so he could continue protecting and defending.

But you never thought beyond that, did you? You never thought there might be something else for you outside violence.

The thought was deeply disturbing and he didn't want to think about it, so he focused on Ivy instead.

'And what was it that you thought you had no chance of getting?' he asked, even though he thought he knew the answer to that already.

Finally, she looked up from her juice, her gaze meeting his. 'A family, Nazir.'

There was such honesty in her gaze, no armour, no evasions. This was the precious heart of her and she was showing it to him.

I was the only one in the home who was never adopted. One by one all the other kids were, including my friend, Connie, but not me. Never me...

She'd told him that days ago. He'd meant to tell

her more about how he wanted her, but then she'd distracted him with talk about his past.

'There was never anything wrong with you, Ivy,' he said quietly, addressing not her statement, but the doubt he could see lingering in her eyes, and the underlying pain that went with it. 'I don't know why you were never chosen to be adopted, but it wasn't due to a failure on your part. You know that, don't you?'

Her lashes fluttered. 'No. I don't know that.' Her voice was husky and uncertain. 'There was one couple who I thought wanted me. They showed me a room they'd prepared for me, talked about how they couldn't wait for me to be their daughter. But it…fell through at the last minute. I was told they'd changed their minds, though not why.'

A sharp, aching sensation caught behind his breastbone, and he was conscious of a simmering anger gathering along with it. At the foolish couple who'd changed their minds, who'd got a lonely child's hopes up then dashed them. He felt anger for her disappointment and her pain. For the self-doubt it had obviously instilled in her.

The intensity of his anger seemed wildly out of proportion to what on the surface was merely a child's disappointment. Except there was nothing 'mere' about it. Not when it had obviously cut her to the bone.

'You really think that was your fault?' He tried to control his tone, tried not to let any of his volcanic fury show.

'I'm not sure who else's it could be. And it wasn't

just that one couple, Nazir. There were others.' Pain rippled across her lovely face. 'I never knew why. And perhaps that was the worst part of all, the not knowing. Because it meant I couldn't do anything about it, couldn't do anything to change it. Couldn't do anything to make myself more... I don't know... more acceptable somehow.'

Nazir couldn't move for the fury burning inside him, at the defeat and self-doubt in her voice. He wanted to hurt the people who'd hurt her, do violence to them, give them pain so they'd never make that mistake again.

Why are you thinking like this? Why are you letting her get to you?

The thought filtered through his anger like a thread of ice. Because he *was* letting her get to him, wasn't he? He was letting her feelings matter, letting *her* matter.

And he couldn't allow it.

Perhaps your control isn't quite as perfect as you think...

The ice became a noose, choking him, and this time it was he who had to look away, fighting to retain his grip on himself. Fighting not to leap up from his seat and find her enemies and vanquish them. Or, better yet, reach for her, drag her across the table, rip her clothes away and show her just how much *he* wanted her. Then wipe that pain from her face for ever, brand himself into her skin, so she knew down to her bones that she was wanted.

'You were always acceptable, Ivy,' he said, fighting to keep his voice level, knowing he was sounding overly harsh yet unable to help it. 'The problem was theirs, not yours. Never yours.'

'Do you really believe that?'

There was such fearful hope in the words that he knew he couldn't keep his gaze away, that he was going to have to look at her and let her see how deeply he believed it. He was going to have to reveal himself to her, even as his logic warned him coldly against it.

But he couldn't not. He couldn't be just another person who hurt her.

So he met her gaze, letting her see the truth, because her own honesty was a gift, a gesture of trust, and he could do no less. 'Yes,' he said, allowing conviction to vibrate in each word so she wouldn't be in any doubt. 'Everything about you is perfect. Your strength and your loyalty. Your passion and your intelligence. Your curiosity, your stubborn determination, and even your fury. Every part of you. Understand?'

She'd gone very still, staring at him, her gaze full of a thousand things he couldn't read, all while the noose around his neck got tighter and tighter.

If you feel this strongly about Ivy, what about your child? How will you feel about him or her?

The question coiled around him, adding another strand to those already wrapped around his throat and pulling tight. Because it wasn't only Ivy who had the potential to test his control over his emotions, the child would too. His child. *Their* child.

You'll feel the same fury. The same need to pro-

tect, to defend. The same jealousy and possessive-
ness, and you will want more and more, and it will
never be enough...

The choking sensation became more intense and
he put the glass back down on the table and was on
his feet before he'd fully thought about what he was
doing.

Ivy stared at him in surprise. 'Nazir? What's
wrong?' The light flickered over her lovely face, illuminating the delicious shape of her body beneath
her robe, and he was suddenly hungrier than he'd ever
been in his entire life.

And not just for sex, but for something deeper,
something richer. Something more.

Something he knew deep down that he didn't deserve to have.

'Nothing's wrong,' he said curtly. 'I merely have
some arrangements to make.'

But an expression of concern crossed her features.
'Is it me? Did I say something I shouldn't?'

'No.' He was sounding harsh, but he couldn't stop
it. 'There are a few things I have to check on for our
upcoming marriage.' He turned towards the doorway
of the villa, away from the table and the flickering
light, and the lovely, warm woman sitting opposite.

'Nazir?'

But he didn't respond. He couldn't. He had to go
and get rid of these feelings somehow, and luckily he
knew exactly what would help.

Without a word, Nazir strode from the terrace
leaving Ivy sitting there alone.

* * *

Ivy stared at the doorway into the house where Nazir had disappeared so suddenly, a familiar anxiety twisting in her gut.

What on earth had happened? Why had he walked away like that?

They'd been having a perfectly lovely dinner, made even lovelier by the things he'd said about her, about how there was nothing wrong with her, that she was perfect. She wasn't sure how he'd managed to guess her underlying fears the way he had, that there'd always been something wrong with her, because why else hadn't she been adopted by anyone?

That self-doubt had eaten away at her for years, though she hated to acknowledge it in any way. Yet looking into his eyes and seeing the conviction burning in them had felt like balm to a festering wound. As if all those people suddenly didn't seem important any more, their opinions about her irrelevant.

Nazir believed she was perfect and that was all that mattered.

Of course, she didn't need validation from anyone, yet she couldn't deny that his meant a great deal to her. In fact, she was starting to think that *he* meant a great deal to her, especially over the past couple of days.

She'd never had someone's sole attention before. Never had anyone put her needs first. Even something as simple as making sure her favourite tea was available and that the food she liked to eat was in supply in the kitchen. She'd never had anyone be interested in her opinions on a subject and want to talk to her about it, or even listen to what she had to say. Or no, that wasn't quite true. She'd had Connie, who'd given her a taste of what friendship was like. But it wasn't friendship she had with Nazir. It was something different, something that felt deeper, that had a physical element, the bond that came with sex and also with the fact that the child inside her was his.

A child she'd been starting to think about as theirs. She hadn't wanted to stop thinking about Connie as the baby's mother because Connie had been the whole reason for its existence. But Connie wasn't here, and, regardless of how the baby had come to be, Ivy would be its mother.

No. She would be *his* mother.

Her hand rested on her stomach, a deep feeling of peace stealing through her, as though she'd come to some kind of agreement within herself. Yes, she would be his mother and Nazir would be his father, and they would be a family together. It was what she'd always wanted—what they'd both wanted, if what he'd said was true.

But…

She glanced again at the doorway, frowning. Something had affected him, causing his expression to harden and his turquoise eyes to ice over.

It's you. You know you're always the problem.

Except no, she didn't think that was true, not this time. They'd been talking about her, it was true, but he'd told her she was perfect, that there was nothing wrong with her, so what had made him suddenly walk away like that?

The Ivy of a week ago would have dismissed it in order to hide her own anxiety that it was something she'd done. But the Ivy she was now was different. The new Ivy had spent a week in his arms discovering that when he smiled he was mesmerising and that he had a playful side she found absolutely delightful. That he was interesting and knowledgeable about the world, having been to a great many places, and hadn't minded one bit her peppering him with questions about them.

The new Ivy could make him growl with need and pant with desire.

The new Ivy could make him burn.

And that Ivy wasn't going to let him walk away from her without finding out what was hurting him.

Taking one last sip of her juice, she got to her feet and moved over to the doorway, the silky fabric of the robe whispering against her bare skin.

She had no idea where he might be, but she checked the usual places: the living area, the terrace, the small, cosy library—though, to be fair, that was her preferred place to be rather than his. He wasn't in the office either, or the bedroom. Which only left one other place that he spent any time in: the gym on the bottom level of the house.

The house was built of stone and there was a timeless quality to it and to the furnishings, but the gym was resolutely modern. It was a big, wide open space, mirrored down one wall and full of different apparatus, treadmills and rowing machines, a stationary bike and an elliptical, weight benches and other constructions built of gleaming steel with bars at different heights.

She found Nazir standing beneath one of these, stripped to the waist. As she paused in the doorway, he raised his arms, made a powerful, graceful leap and caught hold of the bar. He hung suspended there for a couple of seconds, then, with a movement that was nothing but sheer, masculine strength, he began a series of expertly controlled pull-ups.

Ivy leaned against the doorway, watching him.

There was something brutal in the way he moved, in the power and control involved in each pull-up, and it was mesmerising. The lights of the gym highlighted the flex and release of every chiselled muscle, the flat plane of his stomach, the broad expanse of his chest, and the contraction of his biceps as he pulled himself up then let himself down.

He was sleek and immensely powerful, his bronze skin gleaming with sweat.

She swallowed, the ache of desire already building between her thighs. A warrior, that was what he was, a warrior through and through, built to protect. Made to defend.

Yet…that wasn't all he was. There was a compassion to him that she thought he wasn't aware of or that perhaps he tried to hide, and she'd seen the evidence of it in how he spoke of his men and how he ran his army. In how he'd cared for her, too.

What more could he be? What more could he offer

the world beyond skulking out in the desert and hiring an army out for profit? What did he hope to gain by doing it? What was he trying to prove?

Was it all to be a thorn in the side of his half-brother? Or was there more to it than that? Did he believe, as she had, that deep down that was all he was capable of?

Maybe it's all he thinks he deserves?

Well, if so, it wasn't true. And if she could look beyond the home, look beyond the life she'd made for herself that he'd been right to call small, perhaps he could too. Perhaps that compassion of his could be harnessed to his drive to defend and protect, and made into something that could change the world.

He completed the set of pull-ups, letting go of the bar and dropping down onto his feet, wiping his hands of the chalk that had been covering his palms for grip. Without turning, he said, 'I suggest you go and do something else, Ivy. I'll be down here for another hour or so.'

Ivy stared at his powerful back and didn't move.

'Why did you walk away?' she asked.

'I told you. I had some arrangements to make.' He swung his arms, loosening them up in preparation for another set.

'Yes, and I can see that you're very busy making them.'

Nazir turned, his expression set in its usual granite lines, impossible to read as always. But not his gaze. That burned with a fierce, bright light, and it wasn't cold, not now. It was hot, like a fire.

Ivy took a step into the gym, moving towards him, unable to stop herself, drawn relentlessly by that ferocity and that heat. She knew by now what it was: hunger.

He tensed. 'Stop.' His voice was gritty and dark as gravel. 'Stay where you are.'

Ivy paused. 'Why?'

The look in his eyes burned hotter. 'It's better for you not to be around me right now.'

'What do you mean?' she asked, though she suspected she had an idea. 'What's wrong with being around you?'

He stood very still, a seething kind of energy gathering around him. His eyes glittered, his focus predatory. 'You don't want to know.'

Ivy's heartbeat picked up speed, thudding louder in her head as she watched him. He looked dangerous and hungry, like a leopard who'd gone too long without food, and she couldn't shake the feeling that she was the prey he'd just spotted…and that any sudden move would make him pounce.

He doesn't want you close because you threaten his control.

Understanding flickered through her, along with a rush of pure adrenaline, making her breath catch hard. Yes, that was it, wasn't it? And his control was precious to him. He'd always been that way with her, so careful and gentle, and she'd loved that, because it felt good to have someone take care of her.

So you should let him be. Who are you to push him?

But that was a question for the woman she'd been

when she'd first turned up on his doorstep, not the woman she was now. Because the woman she was now wanted more than careful and gentle, and she wasn't going to be put off with excuses about 'arrangements'. He'd released her passion so why couldn't she release his?

Ivy took one step and then another, moving slowly towards him, the fine material of the robe billowing and swirling around her as she walked.

He tensed even more. 'Ivy.'

Her name was a raw command that wouldn't have stopped her in her tracks a week ago and it certainly didn't now. Not when she was so mesmerised by that bright glitter in his eyes, the predatory hunger that was becoming more and more obvious the closer she got to him. Yes, a leopard ready to leap, ready to take down his prey.

But she wasn't his prey. She might be small and she might be pregnant, but she was also his equal, and perhaps it was time he learned that. Perhaps it was her turn to show him that she didn't need him to be careful of her, that he didn't need to be gentle all the time. Perhaps he needed a few lessons on the strength of women.

So she didn't stop. She went right up to where he stood, gleaming with sweat, every line of him hard with carved muscle and radiating raw, masculine strength. Danger gathered around him, a leashed violence that didn't frighten her; it only wound her anticipation even tighter. He was so hot and he smelled

of clean sweat and that dark spice that made her ache
with an intense hunger all her own.

Oh, she wanted him. She wanted him like this,
hungry and desperate, because she'd been hungry
and desperate too. She still was, but only for him.

It will only ever be for him.

The knowledge was like uncovering bedrock under
a mound of loose soil, dense, impossible to shift, and
as heavy as the earth itself. It was a foundation on
which to build her life, because, yes, there would
never be anyone else for her. No other man excited
her, challenged her, fascinated her as he did, and, al-
though it was true that her experience of men was
limited, she had no desire to look further.

Everything she'd ever wanted was standing right
in front of her.

You're in love with him.

Well, obviously. If there was never to be anyone
else, it had to be because she didn't want there to be.
Because this was the man for her, the only man. Was
that love? She had no idea—she'd never been in love
before—but it felt right and true, and she didn't fight
it. Didn't deny it.

She lifted her hand and let her fingers settle in the
hollow of his throat, his skin hot and slick beneath her
touch, the beat of his pulse heavy and sure.

His whole body tensed as she touched him, the fire
in his gaze leaping, sending a pulse of raw electricity
surging through her.

'I'm not afraid of you, Nazir,' she said, meeting
his gaze without flinching. 'So tell me, why should

I keep my distance? What is it exactly that I don't want to know?'

He reached up, his long fingers wrapping around her wrist and holding it. 'You should be afraid.' His hard mouth twisted in what looked like a snarl. 'I can be dangerous when my control is tested. And you test it, Ivy. I don't want to—'

'Hurt me?' she finished, stepping even closer, so they were mere inches apart. 'Don't be stupid. You won't. This isn't about hurting me anyway. This is about the fact that you don't like to be out of control and that's what's really getting to you, isn't it?'

His gaze shifted and glittered, the animal heat in it searing. 'I'm a soldier, little fury. I kill people and I command other men who kill people. You don't want a man like me losing his grip on his control, believe me.'

'But that's not all you are.' She lifted her other hand and put it very deliberately on his chest, feeling the heat of his skin and the beat of his heart against her palm. 'You're not just a soldier and you do more than kill. There's gentleness in you and compassion, and a deep empathy. And I think that was taken from you, wasn't it?'

He bared his teeth, his gaze moving from hers, raking down her body that the robe barely covered. His fingers tightened around her wrist and she could feel his pulse begin to accelerate. 'I don't care about compassion and I care even less about empathy. I'm an animal, Ivy. And right now, if you don't step away I'm going to rip that robe from your body and take you, and there won't be a single thing you can do about it.'

But she only lifted her chin. 'Maybe I want you to be an animal. Maybe I'm an animal too. Did you ever think of that?'

He said something low and rough in Arabic that she didn't understand, his broad chest rising in a sudden, sharp inhale, his heart beating even faster. 'You don't understand. I need to stay in command of myself. I got my mother exiled and my father lost the love of his life. I destroyed my family, Ivy. I don't want to end up destroying you.'

Ivy put back her head and met his fierce, uncompromising gaze. 'Try it,' she said softly. 'See how far you get. I'm tougher than you can possibly imagine.' Then, before he could move, she lifted her fingers from his throat, went up on her tiptoes and pressed her mouth there, tasting the salt and velvet of his skin.

CHAPTER TEN

HER MOUTH WAS like a flame lighting dry touchpaper and Nazir felt the moment he ignited, knew the second he went up like a torch, and he was powerless to stop it.

All the need in him, the possession, the hunger, the desperate desire he'd been holding back for years flooded out of him, tossing aside his precious self-control and drowning him.

Letting go of her wrist, he thrust one hand into her hair and closed his fingers into a fist, dragging her head back and taking her mouth like the conqueror he was.

She didn't protest, didn't cry out, simply surged against him, meeting his kiss as if she'd been waiting for it her entire life.

Foolish, reckless woman. She had no idea what she'd unleashed in him, but it was too late to stop. Too late to hold back. If she wanted him to be an animal then he'd be one and all those things she'd said, about him being compassionate and empathetic, well, she'd soon see those were lies.

He was destruction and he would destroy her.

Her mouth was hot and sweet beneath his and he ravaged it, plunging his tongue deep inside and taking all that sweetness for himself. Still kissing her, he grabbed a handful of her silky robe and pulled hard. The sound of tearing fabric filled the room, but she didn't make a sound. Simply wriggled out of it as he tore it from her then pressed her body against his, all warm, silky female heat.

Everything inside him pulled taut and then snapped, all his hard-earned control, every lesson his father had ever taught him, all his cool logic. They disappeared, drowned under a flood of the most intense lust.

Without thought, he tore his mouth from hers, turned her around in his arms then pushed her face down onto the polished wooden floor of the gym. She gasped, but not in protest, coming up onto her hands and knees, then throwing him the sultriest look over one bare shoulder. It was a dare and a challenge to the predator inside him.

He dropped to his knees behind her, put one hand on the back of her neck, easing her head down onto the floor and holding it there so her cheek rested against the wood, her lovely, heart-shaped rear presented to him. He slipped his free hand between her thighs from behind, stroking through her wet heat to ease a finger inside her, and then, when she jerked and gasped, he eased in another.

She gave the most delicious cry, her back arching, her hips lifting, so he drew his fingers back out then in again, giving her some friction and making her writhe. The feel of her sex clenching around his fingers made him growl in satisfaction and he wanted to keep going, wanted to make her scream with just the movement of his hand. But the ache in his groin was becoming far too intense.

Taking his hand away, he reached for the buttons on his trousers and ripped them open, freeing himself. Then, keeping the pressure on the back of her neck, he thrust hard inside her from behind.

Ivy cried out, twisting on the floor beneath him. She was still up on her knees and he wanted to push her down and cover her entirely like the animal he was, but he had enough presence of mind to know that probably wasn't a good idea considering where their child lay, and so he stayed where he was, satisfying himself with every hard, deep thrust.

He watched her as he moved, as the pleasure gripped him tight. Her face was turned to one side on the floor, her cheeks deeply flushed, thick dark lashes resting on her cheeks. Her mouth was slightly open, deep moans of pleasure escaping her.

She didn't seem to care that she was down on the hard wood, that he had his hand on the back of her neck, that his thrusts were hard, brutal, and savage almost. In fact, if he wasn't much mistaken, she was trying to shove herself back on him, giving him back as good as she got.

Little savage. Little fury.

Little warrior woman.

She is yours. She'll be yours for ever. You will never, ever let her go.

Possessiveness flooded through him and he didn't fight it this time; he let it soak into him, become part of him. He 'd resisted it and resisted it, but there was no resisting any more. She'd unleashed him and here were the consequences.

He drove deeper inside her, feeling her clench around him, stamping his claim on her, making her his in every way there was until the room was full of the sound of her cries and gasps, the sounds of her pleasure and his, until her skin was as slick with sweat as his and she was clawing at the wooden floorboards as if they could give her what she needed.

But they couldn't. Only he could.

He reached around and under her, sliding his hand possessively over the hard roundness of her stomach and down between her thighs, finding the small, hard bud that gave her the most pleasure and he stroked it, teased it.

She shivered and shook, but he kept her pinned, kept pushing deep and hard, kept teasing her with his fingers until he felt her tighten around him, her body convulsing, her scream of pleasure echoing around the room.

It wasn't enough though, so he did it again, pushing her harder, pushing her the way she'd pushed him until she shattered for a second time, and only then did he let himself go, abandoning himself utterly to pleasure as he moved inside her, letting it break him, rip him apart completely then scatter him to the winds.

He lost his grip on himself for some time afterwards and when his awareness returned, he found he'd collapsed on top of her, pinning her curvy little body beneath him. A heavy satiation pulsed through him and he didn't want to move, content to lie there with her beneath him, the scent of feminine musk and jasmine surrounding him. And for a few blissful seconds, he felt nothing but peace.

Then, gradually, he became conscious of what had happened between them, that he'd let his need for her overwhelm him, that he'd let his hunger take control.

You've become everything your father warned you against.

Beneath the sated aftermath of pleasure, the same icy thread that had choked him out on the terrace tightened again, reminding him of what he was, what he'd always be. Not only the by-product of his father's failure to control himself, but also a child full of the same weaknesses. The same needs, the same intense desires. And the same failures too.

Failures that he already knew had had terrible consequences and yet here he was with another failure to add to the list.

Had he learned nothing from his mother's banishment? From how he'd ruined her life and his father's? Had he learned nothing from all the years of perfecting his self-control?

Apparently all it took was one lovely woman to touch him and all those lessons were for nothing.

You can't have her. You don't deserve it.

His heart felt raw and bruised inside his chest, the scent and feel of her flooding his senses, the warmth of her body permeating every part of him. She was a beautiful, strong, vital woman, who matched him in every way possible. And that was the worst part of all.

She was perfect for him, she was everything he'd ever wanted, yet he couldn't have her. Because it was true. He didn't deserve her. His very existence was a mistake, something that shouldn't have happened. His life had brought nothing but sorrow and ruin to both his parents, and he would bring sorrow and ruin to her, too.

In fact, he already had. She was pregnant with his child, a pregnancy she'd only undertaken on behalf of her friend. It wasn't his fault that her friend had died, no, but it was his fault he was keeping Ivy here. It was his fault that he'd demanded she marry him.

She hadn't wanted to; he'd forced her into it.

She never chose you, just as your mother never chose you.

The icy thread, the heavy weight of a shame he couldn't escape, constricted, the beat of his heart loud in his ears.

He should at least have followed the rules his father had tried to instil in him. No children. No wife. No family. No ties to test the weaknesses inside himself. Nothing but cold earth and hard rock, that was his lot in life and he should have accepted it.

He should never have wanted more.

It's not too late. You can save this situation.

Nazir closed his eyes a moment, the knowledge of what he had to do settling down inside him, even as every part of his soul clenched in instinctive denial.

But it had to be done. He must impose distance between them. He had to find his control again somehow and this was the only way.

Carefully, because after all he didn't want to hurt her, he untangled himself and got to his feet. Moving over to where the red robe he'd ripped off her had been discarded, he picked it up and brought it back to her. She'd risen to her feet and so he wrapped the robe gently around her, covering up all that delicious, pale nakedness.

He wished he could savour it a little longer, because he wouldn't see her like this again, but it was better that he didn't. No point in making this any harder than it already was, for him at least.

She smiled at him, her copper gaze full of light and heat, and his heart stumbled in his chest. He hoped this wouldn't hurt her. It might a little, but surely not too greatly. She wasn't here because she wanted to be, after all, but because he'd made her stay.

'I've decided something,' he said, keeping his voice very measured. 'After our marriage, I think you should live here rather than at the fortress.'

She shook her hair back as she adjusted the robe over her shoulders. 'Oh? Why is that?'

'It's quieter, cooler. And the desert is no place for a child.'

She lifted a brow. 'Won't that be too far for you to be from your men?'

'No.' He paused, holding her gaze. 'I won't be living here with you.'

It was the only thing he could do. He had to marry her, had to have his name protecting her and their child, but he couldn't allow himself to stay near her. She was a vulnerability he couldn't allow. Already, it was too much, his control falling by the wayside at one touch of her hand. What would it be like having her around constantly? At his side every minute of the day?

Impossible. His self-control would be dust before the week was out.

Ivy frowned. 'What do you mean you won't be living here with me?'

'I'll live at the fortress where my men are.'

'But—'

'That's my final decision,' he interrupted, because he wasn't going to argue with her about it. 'I have to be where my men are.'

She blinked. 'Oh. Oh, all right, then I'll live there, too. The courtyard is lovely and we can always come here for holidays. The baby will be—'

'No.' He made the word heavy as an iron bar.

'No? What do you mean no?'

'I mean, you and the child will stay here. You'll live here.'

Surprise moved over her delicate features. Then abruptly her gaze narrowed. 'Without you, is that what you're saying?'

He fought the passionate part of himself, turned it

to stone, giving her back the commander of armies, not the man. 'I can't live with you, Ivy.'

'What?' Shock glittered in her eyes. 'Why ever not?'

You have hurt her.

His chest ached, another reminder of how she was getting to him and how severely his control had been compromised. It shouldn't matter that he'd hurt her, it really shouldn't, not when this was better for both of them. Because it would be better for her too, and for their child. That compassion and empathy she'd sensed inside him, that she'd drawn out of him, couldn't be allowed to exist. It compromised him, made him vulnerable. Made him want things he was never meant to have.

And he didn't want to be a father like his own, so cold and hard and emotionally barren. Which meant it was better that he not be anywhere near them.

'Because I'm not going to be the kind of husband you want.' He had nothing else to give her but honesty. 'And I'm not going to be the kind of father our child needs either.'

She looked bewildered. 'I...don't understand. We've been talking for the past week about what our lives are going to look like and how we'd live with you at the fortress and—'

'I know, but I've changed my mind.' He bit out the words, tasting the bitterness in them. Ignoring it. 'It's better for you and for the child to be apart from me.'

She stared at him for a long moment and he could see the hurt glittering in her eyes, a deep and very real hurt that made him ache. 'Why, Nazir? How is it better for our child not to have his father?'

Our child. *His* father. The words caught at his heart like a hook catching on a rock, tugging at him, tearing at him.

He ignored the sensation, shoving it down with all the rest of the weak, shameful emotions he wasn't going to permit himself.

Ivy needed more than an absent husband, especially after the childhood she'd had with the endless rejections and the loneliness. She deserved someone who could give her what she really needed, which wasn't just physical passion, but emotional passion too.

And he couldn't give her that. He'd never be able to give her that.

'Because you both will want something from me that I cannot give you,' he said harshly. 'And since I don't want to hurt you or the child, it's better if I keep my distance.'

A fierce light had begun to glow in her eyes, making him feel a kind of boundless despair. Because of course she wouldn't go without a fight. Of course she wouldn't do what he told her. When had she ever done that?

She was going to make things as hard for them both as she possibly could. She was going to fight him every step of the way, which meant if he was going to protect both of them, he would need to be hard as rock. Obdurate as a granite wall. There could be no weakness in him, no vulnerability, none at all.

Then he would have to deal her a death blow to ensure that she never fought him again.

'So?' Ivy said, staring at him, small and indomitable in her red robe, the light of battle in her eyes. 'What about if I did want something? What if I wanted everything?'

Ivy's heart felt as if it had grown spikes in her chest and they were stabbing into her. Nazir stood in front of her, his powerful body still gleaming with sweat from his workout and then from the intensity of their lovemaking, his features gone hard and impassive as the cliffs outside the villa. His gaze was ice, glittering like a snowfield in the harsh lights of the gym. This was the face of the Commander, cold and implacable, not the hungry desire of the man who'd pushed her to the ground and held her down as he'd taken her rough and hard.

This wasn't the man who'd lost control, who'd been magnificent in his desire, who'd thrilled her right down to her bones with his need for her. She'd loved every minute of it, gloried in every second of how she'd pushed him right to the edge and then over it.

But she should have known there would be consequences, that he wouldn't see his loss of control as an acceptance of their intense chemistry, but as a failure in himself. And that she was something he needed to protect himself from, because of course it wasn't about protecting her and their baby. It was about keeping himself safe.

His set expression didn't change. 'Then you're

going to be disappointed, aren't you? Because there's nothing I can give you.'

A part of her shivered at the indifference in his voice, and it made her want to retreat into her no-nonsense armour. It made her want to put her chin up, draw her robe around her, and tell him she didn't care one way or the other. But that felt like a repudiation of the feeling in her heart, the love that beat strong and sure. Love for the baby inside her and for the man in front of her. Love she couldn't deny or lie about, not any more. Because it was important, too important.

So she didn't retreat, because at heart she was a warrior and always had been, stepping forward instead, coming close to him, inches away from the hot, gleaming bronze of his body. 'And if I told you that I'm in love with you? What would you say then?'

A bright flame flickered in his eyes then died, a fire crushed beneath an avalanche of snow. 'I'm sorry, Ivy. But that won't make the slightest bit of difference.'

She could feel something in her soul tear, an old wound reopening, a wound that had never fully healed and now never would. But she ignored it. This wasn't just about her. It was about the baby she carried too, the baby that needed *both* parents, not only one.

'And your child?' she demanded. 'What about them?'

The expression on his face became even harder. 'The child is why it's even more important that you both live away from me. If you stay I'll ruin you and I'll ruin the child too, and that I can't allow.'

Pain rippled out inside her, but she ignored it, trying to focus on what he was saying. 'What do you mean you'll ruin us?'

'I'm a bastard, Ivy. Evidence of my father's failure to control himself. Evidence of my mother's weakness. I ruined their lives by my very existence.'

'But how is that your fault?'

Fury passed over his granite features, the ice in his eyes shifting a second, allowing her to catch a glimpse of the raw pain that lived beneath the surface. 'If I'd followed the rules, if I'd stayed in control, things might have been different. I could have helped them be together, not driven them apart. But I didn't follow the rules and I didn't stay in control. And in the end, I ensured that they never saw each other again.'

He truly believed that; she could see it in his face. And it made her heart shrivel up in her chest like a flower exposed to frost. 'No,' she said hoarsely. 'You can't take the blame for what happened. That wasn't your fault.'

His expression shut down, the pain gone, leaving only a flat expanse of ice. 'Of course it was my fault. I was the one who lost control of my temper. I was the one who attacked my half-brother. And I was the one who gave away their secret. No one else.'

'But you—'

'Which means that for the rest of my life, I need to live according to the principles my father taught me. To have no children. No wife. No family. No emotional ties whatsoever.'

Her eyes prickled with tears, a deep well of hurt for

him opening up inside her. 'That's not a life, Nazir. That's just…nothing. And I know, because that's what I had until you came along.'

'Then you must be grateful for what you have. You will have our baby and that will surely be enough.'

Her throat closed up, pain like a vice around her heart. 'But it's not and it never will be. You child needs you, Nazir.' She took a breath, then offered up the last piece of her soul. '*I* need you.'

Yet he only gave her back the same expressionless stare. 'A soldier's job is to protect and defend, and that's what I'm going to do. Even if what I have to protect you from is myself.'

Anger bloomed suddenly in the depths of her pain, wrapping around her in a cleansing fire. 'You really think this is about protecting me? Protecting our son?' Her voice cracked, fury laced through it. 'No, I don't accept that. This is about fear. Your fear.'

Finally, heat flickered in his frosty gaze as the barb hit home. 'I'm not afraid.'

'Yes, you are,' she insisted. 'You're terrified. Your mother broke your heart and your father broke your will, and now you can't risk either ever again.' She took a step towards him, now just bare inches away. 'Well? Tell me that isn't true.'

His gaze raked over her, cold, indifferent. 'My heart I cut out years ago and as for my will, my father didn't break it. He created it. He taught me how to keep it strong. I forgot his lessons for a time, but I seem to have remembered them now.'

Tears blurred her vision, her anger receding as

quickly as it had come. 'You keep thinking of love as a vulnerability, Nazir,' she said hoarsely. 'But it isn't. I love you and I love our child and I don't feel vulnerable. I feel strong. I feel like I could climb mountains and conquer the world.'

There were no flickers of heat now, no glimpses of anger or pain. His expression was wiped clean. 'That has not been my experience,' he said without any emphasis at all.

He wasn't going to change his mind, that was obvious. If he wouldn't change it for his child, then he wasn't going to change for her, and she knew it.

Which made her decision very clear.

Ivy swallowed down her agony, grabbed the brightness that had flickered to life inside her, the love for the baby she carried, the love for her best friend who now wasn't here, but who'd been the only person to choose her, and she held onto it tightly.

'In that case,' she said, lifting her chin, 'I can't marry you, Nazir. And we can't live here, exiled to the mountains the way your mother was exiled from Inaris.'

He stared at her, giving her nothing, his gaze darkening, the ice thickening, taking all her rage, all her passion, all her love, and giving her nothing but a cold, black void.

'You're right,' he said without any discernible expression. 'In which case, it's best that you return to England. I will of course provide money for the child and protection for you.'

There were bitter words she wanted to say to him.

Hot, angry words. Words aimed like weapons that would cut him and hurt him the way he was hurting her.

But suddenly she'd lost her taste for a fight. He'd made his decision and, as he'd already told her once before, fighting him would only waste her energy and she was going to need all that energy to care for their baby.

And she would care for it, she knew that deep in her heart. She had all this love inside her and she was desperate to give it to someone, and so she would give it to her baby. She would shower him with so much love he'd never know that his father hadn't wanted him.

'Okay,' she said quietly. 'If that's the way you want it, I'm not going to argue. And I'm not going to fight, not this time.' She lifted her chin and looked him in the eye. 'This is your choice, Nazir, not mine. I would have chosen you if you'd let me.'

Nazir's eyes glittered, his face a mask. 'But I don't want to be chosen, Ivy.' His voice was as cold as the north wind. 'I'm sorry.'

There was nothing to say to that. She'd opened herself up to him, given herself to him and he didn't want her. What could she do about that?

There's nothing you could do. Nobody ever wanted you, remember?

No, but Connie had. And her child would. And even if the man she wanted more than her next breath didn't, she wouldn't be alone.

Ivy swallowed back her tears, swallowed back her pain. She gave him one nod, then she turned on her heel and walked out.

CHAPTER ELEVEN

NAZIR STOOD AT the window of his office, looking out onto the courtyard. The fountain was playing, filling the air with delicate music, and it all looked very peaceful. The gardener was trimming one of the trees, the dry snick of his pruning shears providing a counterpoint to the fountain.

It was a peaceful scene and one that normally he wouldn't even have been aware of, too focused on his army, his men and the operations he was planning. Now, however, it was all he could see, his mind circling around and around the fact that something was missing from it. That there should be a small, determined woman talking to the gardener, her face alight with interest. A small woman with a hot mouth whom he'd kissed there weeks earlier.

A woman he'd let walk out of his life a month ago.

It had been the right thing to do—the only thing to do—so why he should still be thinking about her, he had no idea.

He'd sent with her a couple of his best men to give her discreet protection, as well as contacting the best doctors in England to keep track of her pregnancy. He'd put money in her bank account—money he'd noted she hadn't touched—and had provided everything he could for her.

She was no longer his concern.

Yet over the past month he'd felt strangely hollow, as if he were missing a vital piece of himself, which surely couldn't be right. He hadn't given her anything, so why he should feel as if she'd taken something from him, he had no idea.

One thing he was glad about, though, was that he no longer felt that ache he'd always felt around her.

He didn't feel anything at all, which was quite frankly a relief.

There was conversation behind him, the rumble of male voices obscuring the sound of the fountain, and suddenly, out of nowhere, came an intense, powerful rage.

'Leave,' he ordered sharply, without turning around.

Shock filled the silence behind him.

'But, sir—' someone began.

Nazir turned around, surveying the gathering of his highest-ranking officers with intense distaste. He didn't want these men here. He didn't want this army. He didn't want the heat of the desert or the hardness of the stones. He'd had nothing but rock and stone all his life and he was tired of it.

He wanted to hear the delicate sound of the fountain and the snick of those shears. He wanted to look at the green shrubs and flowers. He wanted…

You want her.

'Get out,' he repeated without raising his voice. 'All of you, get out. Now.'

His men didn't need to be told twice. Within seconds he was alone, the music of the fountain filling the silence of the room.

It should have eased him, but it didn't. It only reminded him of *her*.

Ivy in her transparent red robe. Ivy beneath him, crying out her pleasure. Ivy standing toe to toe with him, fighting him.

Ivy with tears falling down her cheeks telling him that she loved him.

Nazir paced to the meeting table in the middle of the room and put his palms flat on the surface, staring down at the dark grain of the wood.

Why was he constantly thinking of her? He could have understood if they had just been thoughts about her in his bed, her hot mouth and the slick feel of her body around his. But they weren't. He thought about her fighting spirit, the shy way she teased him, the insightful way she viewed things, the excitement when she talked about something that interested her, and the grief that had filled her voice when she'd talked about her friend. The warmth that had suffused every word as she'd spoken about the baby.

Their baby.

His heart felt as if there were an arrow piercing it, a raw, painful wound that he'd spent the past month telling himself he didn't feel. But of course he was wrong. He did feel it.

And it was agony. It was a rent in his soul miles deep. *This is about fear,* Ivy had told him. *Your fear.*

Nazir stared at the table, unable to get the image of her out of his head, standing tall and strong and so very beautiful in front of him.

This is your choice, Nazir, not mine. And I would have chosen you if you'd let me.

But he hadn't let her. He'd made his own choice, telling himself it was about protecting her and their child, about not wanting the stain of his existence to bleed into theirs and ruin them the way he'd ruined his parents.

Perhaps she was right. Perhaps it had been about fear. Yet it wasn't only that.

It was about shame, too.

He was the bastard son of the Sultana, a mistake that had to be kept secret, and he'd been made to feel like that all his life. He'd never been allowed to show his feelings openly, had always had to keep them to himself lest he betray her and his father and their liaison.

And the day he'd forgotten, the day he'd lost control, he'd been punished for it. And so had everyone around him.

His father had always viewed the intensity of his son's emotions as a failure, and so he'd never forgiven Nazir for that final slip, especially when it had lost him the woman he loved. And so the shame had wound its way into Nazir's heart. He was ashamed of himself, ashamed of his feelings, and so he'd got rid of them, purged them like an illness from his body.

And it hit him all of a sudden that that shame was still there, sitting inside him like a canker.

That was why he was here in his iron fortress, skulking in the desert and refusing to leave. Making sure his country was safe but doing it from the shadows, keeping himself a secret, never declaring himself openly.

He never did anything openly.

But she did.

She had. She'd told him she loved him. She'd given away that piece of herself without hesitation, leaving herself so vulnerable. Leaving herself open.

Love has made me strong, she'd said, and at the time he hadn't been able to conceive how love could be a strength, not when he could see the agony burning in her eyes. Yet…now he could see, now it was so very clear.

There was strength in vulnerability, so much strength. Because it took both strength and courage to be vulnerable to someone else, to open yourself up and risk being rejected, risk being hurt.

It was a choice. Ivy hadn't had to risk herself for him; she'd chosen to.

I would have chosen you if you'd let me.

And she had chosen him.

That pierced him to the core. She'd opened herself up and not to just anyone but *to him.* A man who hadn't given her any sign that he felt anything for her but lust. Yet she'd opened her heart, her very soul, to him. She'd trusted him…

And you threw it away.

Nazir closed his eyes, the shame deepening inside him. She'd been open and trusting and honest, and he'd thrown it back in her face. He'd treated her as his father had treated him, as if her feelings meant nothing, as if they were worthless. And that was weak, cowardly.

But then perhaps that was what he'd always been. Weak. Afraid.

So? It's a choice. She found courage and she found strength. Why can't you?

In the darkness behind his closed lids, he could see the choice before him.

He could go on as he had done before, thinking he was strong and skulking in his iron fortress, doing everything in the shadows, still hiding, still ashamed. Still being his father, in essence.

Or he could choose a different path from the one his father had taught him. He could choose to step away from the shadow of shame. He could choose to be vulnerable, to be open. He could choose to give away that last piece of himself.

He could choose love.

He could choose Ivy.

Nazir's eyes flicked open, a wave of the most intense longing flooding through him. Longing for her and her presence. Her warrior spirit. For the child they had created together even though they hadn't known it at the time. For the family he'd always wanted that, deep in his heart, he'd never thought he deserved.

But this time he didn't push it away, he let it fill

him. Let it wash away the shame and the hurt. The betrayal and sorrow.

And he smiled, because she was right, his little fury. She'd always been right. Love wasn't a weakness, it was a strength. He could move mountains with this feeling; he could conquer worlds.

Not that he wanted to. The only conquering he wanted to do involved the demons in his heart, and then maybe he'd give that heart to the woman he'd probably fallen for the moment he'd first seen her.

She might not want him any more. He might have hurt her too badly. But no one had ever chosen her, and so he wanted her to know that he would. That he would give her what he could, that he would give her every last piece of himself and if she trod every piece under her little foot, then that would be no less than he deserved.

Nazir pushed himself away from the table.

It was time he stopped skulking.

It was time to step out of the fortress in which he'd been hiding and into the light.

'Miss Dean!' One of the youngest of the current collection of teenagers in Ivy's home suddenly charged into her office, his eyes very wide. 'There's a huge car out in the street. And it's stopped just outside!'

Ivy looked up from the spreadsheet she'd been going over, rubbing at her temples. She had a headache and the past month of no sleep was catching up with her.

She wasn't sure what was worse, not being able to

sleep because she missed Nazir, or the way he filled
her dreams when she finally managed to get to sleep.
Either way, it was bad.

'What is it, Gavin?' She tried not to sound sharp.
'What do you mean a big car?'

The boy rushed to the window that overlooked the
street, stabbing an urgent finger at it. 'Look!'

Ivy sighed and pushed herself out of her chair,
moving over to the window, because it was clear
Gavin wasn't going to let this go.

Then she stopped, her heart nearly exploding in
her chest.

A long black limousine had pulled up to the kerb
and several people were getting out, including guards
in smart black and gold uniforms. There were four
of them, two standing on either side of the path up
to the front door of the home, while a third stared up
and down the street, obviously looking for danger. A
fourth pulled open the door of the limo.

Several groups of kids that had been playing on
the side of the road stopped and stared. A crowd of
teenagers drinking RTDs, vaping and listening to
tinny dance music on a stereo stopped shouting and
gawped.

The whole world stood still.

It wasn't. It couldn't be…

A man got out of the limo, so tall and broad there
was no mistaking him. He wore the same uniform as
the guards, except the only gold on his was a pin at
his breast, a stylised sun.

He was the most magnificent thing Ivy had ever

seen. Certainly the most magnificent thing her little borough had ever seen.

Her eyes filled with tears as he glanced up at the home, the last in a terraced housing estate in one of London's more depressed areas. Because it was him; of course it was him. Those harshly beautiful masculine features, those cold turquoise eyes.

Nazir.

'Is he a king?' Gavin asked, staring in rapt fascination. 'He looks like a king. What's he doing here?'

Ivy's heart was beating very, very fast, longing almost strangling her. 'A good question,' she said hoarsely. 'A very good question indeed.'

Why? He'd sent her away; he'd let her go. She'd offered him her heart and he hadn't wanted it. And she'd spent the past month in agony because of it.

She stepped away from the window and went back to her desk, her throat thick, her mouth dry. Perhaps if she ignored him, he'd go away?

Someone knocked loudly on the front door.

'I'll answer it,' Gavin shouted and raced off before she could tell him to stop.

She sat there, her heart quivering in her chest, her eyes full of tears, anger and love warring for precedence inside her. She didn't want to see him. She didn't want to see him ever again.

The sound of voices came from the hall, deep, masculine voices, and then Gavin was back again, leading a group of black-clad guards with Nazir at the head, straight into Ivy's office.

'Here she is,' Gavin announced, pointing triumphantly at Ivy. 'There.'

And Ivy found herself staring straight into Nazir's turquoise eyes.

He didn't look anywhere else, only at her. 'Thank you,' he said to Gavin. 'Go with my men, please. They have things for you.'

'Things?' Gavin looked suspicious. 'What things?'

'If you want to know, you'll have to go with them, won't you?'

Within seconds the boy was gone, the guards closing the doors after them as they went out of the room, leaving her and Nazir alone.

For a second nothing happened. The room was full of a thick, seething tension.

Then, much to her shock, Nazir dropped to his knees in front of her desk.

Ivy stared at him, open-mouthed. 'What…what are you doing?' Her voice was breathy with pain and shock.

He stared straight at her and there was no ice in his eyes now, no expanse of snow. They burned hot, clear, and fierce. 'I'm here to offer you everything I am, Ivy Dean. My army, my fortress, my money, and every last piece of myself. They're all yours.'

She blinked, feeling as if she could hardly breathe. 'What do you mean?'

His eyes glittered, his expression slowly changing into one of stark longing. 'I mean, I've tried, little fury. I've tried to live the way my father taught me. I've tried to live with nothing. Wanting nothing. And

I just can't seem to do it any more. You were in my thoughts constantly. I kept reaching for you at night. I couldn't look at the courtyard in the fortress without seeing you, without wishing I could see you. Without wanting you desperately.'

Slowly, Ivy rose to her feet, every part of her shaking. 'I don't understand. You sent me away. You said—'

'I was wrong,' he interrupted, his deep voice vibrating with emotion. 'I was wrong about everything and you were right. It was fear that kept me from you, Ivy, but not only that, it was shame too. I've been my parents' shame for years, the secret that must be kept hidden. And I could never show my feelings, never let them out in case I betrayed them, and my father never let me forget it.' A muscle jumped in the side of his jaw. 'I was ashamed of myself. Ashamed of my feelings. And control was the only way to deal with that. But…you were never ashamed, little fury. You embraced your feelings and showed them to me with strength and courage. And you showed me that it was a choice. That I could choose a better life, one without shame or fear.' There was naked longing on his face now, the sharpness of it shocking her. 'A life with you in it. And so that's why I'm here. I'm here to choose you, Ivy. And I know you may have changed your mind about me, but I wanted to tell you that I love you. You have every piece of my heart, every piece of my soul.'

She was shaking. Shaking so hard she couldn't stop. 'But—'

'I'm going to give up my army. I'm going to give up skulking in the desert and making things difficult for Fahad and Inaris. I've decided to buy a house in London and I'll be living there. If you don't want to see me, you don't have to. But I'd dearly love to be able to see my child if—'

But she didn't let him finish. Somehow, she found her strength and was around the side of her desk, striding over to where he knelt on her threadbare carpet. She took his face between her hands and stopped his words with her mouth.

For a single shining minute both of them froze at the connection, at the heat and flash fire of it, the sweetness and the deep familiarity. The sense of coming home, of being safe. Of being loved.

Then Nazir surged to his feet and she was in his arms, surrounded by his strength and his heat, held secure and protected as the kiss deepened, intensified. She could taste his longing, his need, and he didn't hold back, didn't hide it. And so she gave it back to him, letting him know that this was what she wanted, that he was what she'd always wanted.

'No,' she whispered against his mouth. 'I haven't changed my mind. And yes, I want every piece of you, just like you have every piece of me. I love you, Nazir. And you don't have to give up anything for me. I want you just as you are, armies and fortresses and skulking and all.'

He kissed her again, deeper, harder. And gradually Ivy began to be aware of a commotion outside her office, a very happy-sounding commotion. She pushed at Nazir's broad chest. 'What's going on out there?'

His eyes glittered. 'I brought the kids a few gifts. That will keep them occupied while I keep you occupied.'

A fierce, bright happiness lanced through her even as she blushed scarlet. 'Really? Here? Now?'

'Yes.' He looked as if he wanted to devour her whole. 'Really. Right here. Right now. Lock the door, little fury. Let me show you how much I love you.'

So she did and he showed her.

And in his arms she found what she'd been looking for her whole life.

A home. A family. And most important of all, she found love.

EPILOGUE

IVY WENT INTO labour just as she and Nazir had come in from a nice, long stroll around one of the most picturesque villages in Italy's Cinque Terre. Instantly, he mobilised the small medical team he had on standby, much to her annoyance since she was only having a baby, not a serious medical event.

He ignored her, managing the move to the hospital and everything in between. Eventually, though, he ran out of things to manage and was forced to do nothing but be at her side, holding her hand, unable to do a single thing as she gave birth to their son.

It seemed she was right about that too. He was, indeed, a boy.

Much, much later, as Nazir cradled his newborn son in the crook of his arm while he cradled his wife in the other, he felt a contentment steal through him unlike anything he'd ever felt in his entire life.

He'd given up his army, had handed it over to his second-in-command and the fortress with it, and he and Ivy now headed a worldwide charitable organisation dedicated to the well-being of at-risk children. He had no regrets. None whatsoever.

'So,' he said softly into the silence. 'How do you feel about a daughter?'

Ivy groaned. 'To be honest, I feel it's in very poor taste to start talking about another child when I've only just had this one.' But after a moment, she snuggled against him. 'As long as we call her Connie.'

Nazir had no issues with that. Nor did he have any issues when Connie came with a twin sister they called Cora. Or with the little boy who came along a few years later as an extra-special surprise.

Because he wasn't a vicious warlord any more or an unwanted bastard son. Or a lonely man hiding in the desert in a fortress with gates of iron.

He was the husband of Ivy Al Rasul and the father of four beautiful children.

And he wanted nothing more.

* * * * *

#3929 MARRIED FOR ONE REASON ONLY
The Secret Sisters
by Dani Collins

A few stolen hours with billionaire Vijay leaves Oriel with a life-changing surprise—a baby! He demands marriage...but can she really accept his proposal when all they've shared is one—albeit extraordinary—encounter?

#3930 THE SECRET BEHIND THE GREEK'S RETURN
Billion-Dollar Mediterranean Brides
by Michelle Smart

When tycoon Nikos emerges from being undercover from his enemies, he discovers he's a father. He vows to claim his son. Which means stopping Marisa's business-deal marriage and reminding her of *their* electrifying connection.

#3931 A BRIDE FOR THE LOST KING
The Heirs of Liri
by Maisey Yates

After years presumed dead, Lazarus must claim the throne he's been denied. But to enact his royal revenge, he needs a temporary fiancée. His right-hand woman, Agnes, is perfect, but her innocence could be his downfall...

#3932 CLAIMING HIS CINDERELLA SECRETARY
Secrets of the Stowe Family
by Cathy Williams

Tycoon James prides himself on never losing control. It's what keeps his tech empire growing. As does having his shy secretary, Ellie, at his side. So their seven nights of red-hot abandon shouldn't change anything...until they change *everything*!

HPCNMRA0721

#3933 THE ITALIAN'S DOORSTEP SURPRISE
by Jennie Lucas

When a mesmerizing and heavily pregnant woman arrives on his doorstep, Italian CEO Nico is intrigued. He doesn't know her name but can't shake the feeling they've met before...and then she announces that the child she's carrying is his!

#3934 FROM ONE NIGHT TO DESERT QUEEN
The Diamond Inheritance
by Pippa Roscoe

Star awakens a curiosity in Sheikh Khalif that he hasn't felt since a tragic accident made him heir to the throne. But surrendering to their attraction is risky when duty decrees he choose country over their chemistry...

#3935 THE FLAW IN HIS RED-HOT REVENGE
Hot Summer Nights with a Billionaire
by Abby Green

Zachary hasn't forgotten Ashling's unparalleled beauty—or the way she almost ruined his career ambitions! But when chance brings her back into his world, Zach discovers he wants something far more pleasurable than payback...

#3936 OFF-LIMITS TO THE CROWN PRINCE
by Kali Anthony

When Crown Prince Alessio commissions his portrait, he's instantly enchanted by innocent artist Hannah. She's far from the perfect princess his position demands. But their dangerous desire will make resisting temptation impossible...

YOU CAN FIND MORE INFORMATION ON UPCOMING HARLEQUIN TITLES, FREE EXCERPTS AND MORE AT HARLEQUIN.COM.

HPCNMRB0721